Bulletface 4: The Cc

Written by, Rio

This is a work of fiction. Any resemblance to actual persons (living or dead), or references to real people, events, songs, business establishments, or locales is purely coincidental. All characters are fictional, and all events are imaginative.

Bulletface 4: The Cocaine King

Copyright © 2015 by Rio Terrell

** Acknowledgements

Thank you God. For everything.

Mom, Annette, and Pops, Prentice, I love you both until the end of time.

Kenneth, you never turned your back on me my whole bid. I love you to life, big bruh. Delilah too. And Dekenta and Deante.

To my readers: Pam and Quateisha Williams (RIP John P. Williams), Kesa Muhammed (one of my day one readers), Melonie Frazier, Judy Richburg, Isyces Cubes, Jenell Proctor, Farshawna Crook, Keisha Johnson, Latasha Mack, (my literary sisters) Shelli Marie, Ellen Sade, and Teruka Carey; Nikolai Konstantin, Terrineka Jones, Summer Grant, Michelle Sanford Harvey, Cynthia Scott, Jennifer Williams, Ranada Lewis, Beverly Jackson, Allisha Bethel, Sunshyne Kiss, Lorianne Tillman, Shontelle Evette, Tyrin Libertowski, Shannon Lyttle, Donica, and everyone else. If I forgot you, put your name here _____. I appreciate each and every one of you.

To the many newcomers to the publishing industry, I wish you all the success in the world. My best advice is both simple and difficult— never stop writing.

God bless.

** Dedication

In loving memory of Verna Jones.

Prologue

February 14th, 2015
Casa Casuarina (The Versace Mansion)

Scantily clad in a white lace and mesh Victoria's Secret teddy over seven-inch Christian Louboutin heels of the same color, bejeweled in more than $2 million in precious white diamonds, Alexus Costilla did a twirl in front of the mirror in her walk-in closet, admiring her jaw-dropping curves, her small waist, her massive derrière. Beyoncé's "Flawless" was playing from the many speakers that were embedded in the ceilings throughout the lavish Miami Beach mansion.

"Who's badder than me?" she said, smiling at her reflection and wiggling her thighs ever so slightly to cause the ripple effect that her now hospitalized husband, Blake "Bulletface" King, loved so much.

She was a dime piece with a net worth of $85 billion and an additional $148 billion in dirty money. She was a corporate business mogul and a quick-tempered Mexican drug cartel boss, as famous as Beyoncé Knowles and as deadly as Gakirah Barnes, legendary in Mexico and an urban legend in America.

On top of it all she was a depressed mother who'd recently miscarried what would have been her second child.

She heard the bedroom door open and watched Enrique, her head of security, walk into the room wearing an indecipherable expression over a snow-white Hartmarx suit. He had an unlit Cuban cigar stuffed in the corner of his mouth, and his eyes were on his iPhone.

He didn't speak; instead, he offered Alexus his smartphone, and she felt her heart drop to her stomach as she grabbed it and began reading.

It was a TMZ article.

'Bulletface sextape leaked, and it's not with Alexus!'

Alexus's gentle smile became an angry scowl. She read on:

'An hour-long sextape of rapper Bulletface and Porsche Clark, Mercedes Costilla's younger sister, has just been leaked online...'

"Oh, my God, are you serious!" Alexus shouted. She hurled the phone onto her bed and gave Enrique an icy stare.

"Hey," Enrique said, raising his hands in surrender. "We already assumed she'd drugged him that day in Atlanta. That's what it looks like in the video. He's completely out of it, hardly moving, not speaking. I believe she did drug him. Probably slipped it in that Codeine he's always drinking."

"I asked that bitch..."

"Yeah, but you know she's not going to admit to that. You'd kill her."

Alexus gritted her teeth, and her nostrils flared as she glanced at the smartphone. It had landed on its back. Its glowing screen taunted her.

"Where is Porsche?"

"We can't kill her. The media's all over this story. Let things simmer down a little. I'll do her myself."

"I want her dead today."

"That would be reckless and you know it."

"Where is Porsche?" she repeated sternly.

"In Barbados. You know she's dating that Bulls player. Think he took her there on a date for Valentine's Day."

Alexus clenched her teeth tightly together and

glowered at Enrique's smartphone for a long moment.

"I don't care what the media will think," she said finally. "Send somebody to blow her lying little head off. Now!"

**Chapter 1

Even with the full-length black mink coat sheltering her rich brown skin from the blistering Windy City weather, Mercedes Costilla was still a little too cold for comfort as she, her eight-man security team, and her new boyfriend, Biggs, marched toward her brand-new triple-black Rolls-Royce Phantom. The car was a gift from her billionaire sister Alexus; the bodyguards were necessary because of her billionaire sister Alexus, for numerous reasons.

She'd just squandered $184,947.15 on a Michigan Avenue shopping spree, which explained the fifteen bags her bodyguards were carrying and the sparkling gold and diamond Cartier watch on her wrist.

Last week's Forbes magazine had listed her net worth as $20 million, but in all actuality she only had $5.2 million in her Chase Bank account, a million-dollar condo here in downtown Chicago, a wardrobe worth about the same, and more than $7,000,000 in drug money in a safe at the Miami mansion she and Biggs had been living in for the past few months.

They wouldn't be in Chicago for long. One more stop and back to the warmth of south Florida.

"That bitch better have our money," Biggs said with a laugh. He was always laughing about something, though Mercedes knew that he could get real gangster in an instant. His itchy trigger finger had saved Blake's life during the shooting that now had Blake hospitalized. Mercedes and Biggs had started dating shortly after the shooting and she hadn't left his side since. He was far too handsome not to give chase— Tall, brown-complexioned, and replete with bulging muscles— and she hoped the groupies that came with the fame of being close friends with Hip Hop's first family wouldn't fuck up the bond they had.

"She'll have it," Mercedes said. "Fanny never comes short. She owns a bunch of car lots, and her little sister is one of the most popular strippers in Atlanta. Trust me, she'll have the money ready as soon as we walk into that restaurant. We'll eat, chit-chat, and leave with the bag."

"We gon' stash that, too. Just keep stackin'."

"What else is there to do?" Mercedes asked. While a few of the bodyguards loaded the bags into their triple-black Escalade, she put on her sexiest smile and wrapped her arms around Biggs's heavy white leather Pelle jacket. She felt the guns he was packing in twin shoulder holsters and the long 30-round clips in his jackets' inside pocket, and the rigid bulletproof vest he never left home without. "Let's fly to Paris tonight. Or Rome. Alexus said Rome is beautiful. She's been there twice."

"We gotta hit the room first." He gave Mercedes a suggestive grin and palmed the meaty cheeks of her ass in his strong brown hands. The air was so cold that clouds of breath escaped his perfect lips as he spoke.

"I love you already, Biggs."

"Show me when we get to the room. Come on, get in the car."

He let her slide into the Rolls first, and then he got in next to her and their driver shut the door. He bit his lower lip and studied her lovestruck expression. Just having a man as handsome and gangster as Biggs warmed Mercedes's heart to no end.

Her attention went to her iPhone as it began ringing. Biggs started kissing the side of her neck before she could answer it, and she decided to let it go to voicemail. The feel of his warm breath under her ear drove her wild, but she managed to keep herself under control.

"Boy, stop," she said, shoving him off her and

planting a quick kiss on his mouth. "Ain't you supposed to be calling Blake?"

"It's Valentine's Day. All I'm supposed to be doin' is pleasing you," he replied, but already he was pulling out his smartphone to call Blake's hospital room.

The sleek black Rolls-Royce glided away from the curb and began its journey up Michigan Avenue. Mercedes shut the curtain over her window and turned on Nicki Minaj's "The Pinkprint" album, gazing out of the corner of her eye at Biggs as he held the phone to his ear. She studied his sharp features, his handsome tan face, his ever-present smirk, and found herself thanking God for sending such a blessing her way. Kenny, her ex-husband, had been a terrible choice, but Biggs seemed like the real deal. He was everything she'd ever wanted in a man: strongly-built, easy on the eyes, gangster, loyal, and well put together. It didn't hurt that Blake had put him on and signed him to Money Bagz Management. He was a millionaire and hadn't even dropped a mixtape yet, fresh out of the fed joint with connections all across the states.

She looked at her own iPhone. The missed call was a Facetime request from Porsche, her younger sister, who was currently in Barbados with an NBA star she'd recently started dating.

This bitch don't want nothin', Mercedes thought as she returned the Facetime call.

Porsche answered and immediately said: "Shit, Mercedes. Shit. I'm dead."

The panic in Porsche's shaky voice and sprightly brown eyes instantly changed Mercedes's disposition.

"What are you talking about, Por—" Mercedes started.

"That sextape I made with Blake, when I drugged him. It's out. Some hacker cracked into the cloud and sent the sextape to everybody. It's on TMZ, World Star Hip Hop, Media Takeout — everywhere."

Mercedes gasped. "Alexus is going to kill you." Tears sprouted up over her worried green eyes. "I told you to delete that video! Why'd you do it in the first place?! Alexus is a fucking cartel boss! Thee biggest cartel boss! Are you really that slow? How am I supposed to save you from this? Huh? We've lost our mother, I lost my kids and their father, and now I'm about to lose you. Thanks a lot, Porsche. I really needed this."

Suddenly they were both sobbing.

"Stop saying that!" Porsche said. "I'm not gonna

die! Stop it. Just stop it, okay? I have two bodyguards here with me now. I'll be fine. Just stop saying —"

A sudden burst of gunfire startled Mercedes.

Porsche screamed, "Oh, my God, Cedes, they're shooting at ME!"

Then the call dropped.

All Mercedes could do was stare at the phone screen with her mouth agape.

Biggs had been paying attention; he draped a strong arm around her shoulders and hugged her tight against his chest.

****Chapter 2

Porsche felt the sting of a bullet tearing through her shoulder as she dove under the table, praying that her bodyguards would draw their weapons before she caught any more bullet wounds. She'd watched the two Hispanic men as they entered the restaurant, automatically thinking that they were members of the Costilla Cartel. Her heart had drummed as the heavier of the two reached in his suit jacket and drew a submachine gun.

She'd gasped when he aimed it at her.

She and her boyfriend — Chicago Bulls point guard Rodney "Hot Rod" Earl— were at The Tides, a five-star restaurant on the sandy beach of Holetown, Barbados. She had on her best dress: a gray, one-shouldered Valentino she'd purchased for this exact date. It showed an eyeful of cleavage and had a sexy slit up the left side.

Now the dress was bloodied. Gunfire was exploding all around her. People were yelling in panic. Dishes were shattering. Tables were overturning.

All hell was breaking loose in the middle of paradise.

"Rodney!" Porsche screamed as a corpulent white businessman in a sharp white suit fell dead beside her table with a hole in both sides of his head.

Rodney appeared at her side just as the gunfire ceased. He snatched her up in his arms and rushed out of the restaurant among a throng of frightened faces. Porsche saw one of her bodyguards lying dead near the front door. Several more men were stretched out disproportionately on the floor in burgeoning pools of blood.

"They were gunning for us," Rodney said, half out of breath as he reached his rented Lamborghini Gallardo and snatched open the passenger door.

"No," Porsche corrected, squinting against the stinging sensation in her right shoulder as Rodney carefully set her down on the passenger seat, "they were gunning for me."

****Chapter 3

Blake grunted and groaned in agony as he struggled forward on the walker, gripping it tightly in both hands and looking at the bathroom door as if he'd never reach it. His iPhone was ringing on the bedside table — Biggs was calling— but Blake was too drugged up and full of pain. He'd call back.

His top-floor room was the largest in Jackson Memorial Hospital. A twelve-man crew of bodyguards, four personal nurses, two personal doctors, and two physical therapists were assigned to the floor specifically to tend to him and only him.

He'd been shot seven times several months prior, and after 37 days in a coma and weeks of strenuous therapy he was back on his feet and moving around on his own.

With the help of the walker, of course. He didn't need it as much as he used it. He was just biding his time until he was strong enough to hit the gym. He knew it would only take around five months to get back to the chiseled form he'd been before the shooting.

This morning the room was void of doctors and nurses. Only the two therapists — a heavyset black woman with red hair named Ms. Eden and a slender Asian woman named Lisa— and four of the bodyguards were in the spacious room with him. The others were somewhere else on the floor, probably smoking, watching television, or phoning their significant others for Valentine's Day.

Ms. Eden and Lisa were guiding him to the bathroom, Ms. Eden who liked him just a little too much and Lisa who always found it hilarious.

He had to piss like a racehorse.

Lisa said: "You should maybe leave that gangster life alone. To live. You can't keep getting shot and expecting to survive. Nobody's invincible."

"Girl," Ms. Eden said, "Blake is like 50 Cent used to be. He's in the streets, ain't that right, Blake? Boy's been shot twenty-somethin' times altogether. He's Bulletface. Sexy, chocolate, the-best-rapper-ever Bulletface. Hell, the name alone—"

Blake turned to the chubby black woman and silenced her with an ice-cold stare. "I'm not tryna hear nothin' right now, a'ight? I just wanna use the bathroom and get back to that bed. Can you be quiet until then?"

Lisa cracked a smile and choked back a laugh, and Ms. Eden sucked her teeth, but neither of the women spoke. Lisa smelled like oranges. She was cute and rail-thin but attractive nonetheless. Ms. Eden was charcoal-black and ogrish but she too smelled sweetly appealing. Whenever he needed to take a leak, Lisa usually helped by freeing his manhood from the navy-blue hospital slacks and aiming it into the toilet, but this time Ms. Eden tried to do it.

He slapped her hand away.

"I got it," he said.

Lisa giggled. Eden shook her head, displaying a guilty grin, and put her hands on her hips.

The two women watched him as he began relieving his bladder. Four bottles of water, two cups of orange juice, and a Pepsi from the night before made for a long piss. He shut his eyes for a brief moment and listened to the splash of urine hitting the toilet water, thinking of nothing in particular. His daughter Savaria's Colgate smile flashed in his mind, followed by the smile of King Neal Costilla, his son.

When he opened his eyes, the therapists were outside the bathroom and his wife was standing in the doorway wearing nothing but a white-lace teddy and heels. She had a gold bottle of Ace of Spades in one hand, and what looked to be an ounce of Kush in the other.

He grinned, suddenly intrigued. Alexus hadn't been to see him since her miscarriage two months ago, back when he'd still been bedridden; seeing her now had him ready to try for another pregnancy.

"You know I'm not supposed to be drinkin'. Shit ain't good for my wounds."

"Who said anything about you drinking? This is my loud and my bottle of Ace. Fuck you. I'd shoot you if I hadn't married you."

"Shoot me?" He frowned discontentedly and slowly reached forward to flush the toilet. "You wanna shoot me on Valentine's Day? What kinda shit is that? And why the fuck you ain't been up here to see me?"

"It's my kinda shit. Cheat on me again and you'll see what I mean." She turned away and walked to his bed and sat down. Casting a salacious smirk his way, she added: "If you want your V Day present I'd suggest you get over here."

"When did I cheat on you?" he asked as Alexus motioned for the therapists to help him back to the bed. He shrugged off their hands and strolled at his own turtle-speed pace. The dose of pain medicine he'd taken shortly after breakfast was taking effect: he could no longer feel the tingling pain on and around the seven gunshot wounds. Though his body was weak, he knew he was capable of protecting himself. He had trust in the Mac-11 submachine gun that was dangling from his neck on a Louis Vuitton shoulder-strap. A chunky white diamond pinkie ring blinged on his left hand. It was as icy as the gold necklace he was wearing and its attached MBM pendant; the Hublot Classic Fusion Haute Joaillerie "$1 Million" watch on his right wrist and the white diamond bracelet on his other wrist. Though he wouldn't admit it, his diamonds were everything to him. The bling signified strength in all matters. He was the king of Hip Hop and Alexus was the wealthiest trap queen in history. Their diamonds said it for them.

He made it to the bed and sat next to her, while Enrique ushered the bodyguards and therapists out of the room.

Eyeing her impeccably manicured fingernails, Alexus said, "We had a drone following you in Miami the day you were shot. I know all about Lakita and Shay."

"I didn't fuck wit' Shay."

"Yeah, but you sure fucked Ki—"

"Hold up," Blake interrupted, frowning. "Drones? That means those drones saw who shot me. And what the fuck are you following me with drones for?"

"You seriously wanna make this about me?" Alexus got up and stood in front of him with her hands on her hips.

"Who shot me?"

"We got them. And I just sent   after Porsche about that sextape. Can't believe she actually drugged you, raped you, and recorded the shit. I suspected she drugged you, but this no good slut had the audacity to suck and ride you like she was me. I'm killing that bitch." Alexus pulled her iPhone6 Plus out of a white leather Birkin bag she'd set on the bedside table. She typed and handed him the phone. It was on a liveleak.com internet bookmark. The caption read "Four men riddled with bullets outside Miami strip club."

Blake clicked on the link. The video began with a group of masked gunmen exiting a black Range Rover and running toward a dark blue Ferrari that was parked in front of King of Diamonds, a strip club Blake and his crew frequented every time they visited Miami.

The gunmen opened fire on two men with

dreadlocks in the Ferrari, and the crowd of club-goers scattered, screaming and running wildly. Two men who'd been leaning against a black Bentley coupe behind the blue Ferrari attempted to draw their guns and were shot down a half second later.

"I recorded that from the backseat of my Phantom," Alexus said cheerfully. "I've had the video for a while now, we got their asses the same night you were shot. Then I had T-Walk sniped two days later." She took the phone back and set it on the table, then unwrapped a Swisher's Sweet cigar, split it down the middle, and filled it with buds of Kush.

Blake ogled her amazing figure while she rolled, wondering what "sextape" she was referring to and guessing it was from when he'd been drugged by Porsche in Atlanta one night following an MBM concert at the Georgia Dome.

"So," he said in disbelief, "the bitch really got me."

"Shouldn't have been having that hoe around you in the first place." Alexus's jaw muscles flexed as she gritted her teeth and flicked open a diamond-encrusted Chanel lighter. She dried the thick blunt and lit it.

Blake grinned at her belligerent expression. He missed seeing her attitudes, and he was surprised she hadn't come to the hospital and shot him dead when she'd learned of his moonlight tryst with Lakita "Bubbles" Thomas.

"Don't be havin' no drones followin' me and shit," he said, raising a hand to rub the generous curves of his wife's derrière. She let him grope to his liking.

Her signature perfume — Clive Christian's Imperial Majesty, $215,000 a bottle — filled his nose with a small piece of heaven.

She blew smoke in his face. "They say you can come home today."

"Why I wanna come home to a wife who ain't been to see me in God knows how long? I'm good here."

"Your little sextape with Porsche is all over the internet."

"So what? The fuck I'm supposed to do about that?"

"I should fuck you up, Blake. You could've stopped her or something."

Blake gave her an incredulous look. "You can't be serious, Alexus. I was drugged up, dummy. Let me drug you up and see what you can do."

Another suck of the teeth. She inhaled a lungful of smoke. Blake lay back on the bed, unable to unglue his eyes from her jaw-dropping curves. She had a black Balmain outfit with matching Louboutin sneakers and ten $10,000 packets of bank-new hundreds stacked next to her fur robe at the foot of the bed for him. On the easy chair in the corner was a Louis Vuitton bulletproof vest and a matching duffle bag.

"I still should fuck you up." Alexus poked the tip of a fingernail into the center of his forehead and gave a weak push. "Keep your dick in your pants. How hard is that? I give you the world. I don't deserve to be cheated on again and again. It gets old, Blake. Fast. Make up your mind. Either you want this marriage to work or you don't."

"You know I love you, baby. Chill out. Get over here." He tried reaching for her but winced as a bolt of pain lanced through his arm.

"I am so serious, Blake. If you fuck one more bitch I'm killing you. One more, you understand? Think I'm playing if you want."

"You ain't supposed to be smokin' loud in a hospital."

"I'm Alexus Costilla, I can do whatever I feel like doing." She hopped onto his lap, and again he winced. "Aww, I'm sorry, did that hurt?" Her voice was full of sarcasm.

Blake pinched her thigh as hard as he could and chuckled as she yelped and slapped him across the face.

"Asshole!" she snapped.

"You love me, though."

"Not as much as you think. Fucker." She lowered her mouth to his and sucked his bottom lip, then kissed him and put his hands on her ass. "Porsche's gonna die for what she did to you. I sent some men to pay her a visit in Barbados."

"You should wait. They'll automatically assume the hit came from you."

"I don't care. Fuck that bitch, and fuck Mercedes, too. They were probably in on it together."

Blake shook his head. "Call off that hit. Mercedes will go nuts if she loses another family member."

"Too late. I sent them three hours ago. They've already touched down in Barbados." Alexus began kissing him, long, passionate kisses that made his heart swarm with emotion and his dick swell with blood. "I love you, boy. Not sure why but I know I do."

"Same here."

"You don't fucking love me."

"Yes, I do."

"How much?"

"A lot."

"How much is a lot?"

"I love you more than anything in the world. You're my wife." He sat up to press his lips to hers as she blew out a stream of smoke.

Then Enrique barged into the room and ruined the mood, holding his gold-plated AK-47 firmly in one hand and his smartphone in the other.

"The two semis we sent to San Fran this morning were just robbed. Our men were killed. We've got video. They were some of T-Walk's guys. The Gangster Disciples. They got off with twelve thousand kilos." He spoke casually, as if twelve thousand kilos was nothing. "And your mother's here with the little ones. Savaria wants another pony." He chuckled dryly.

Alexus picked up the robe and covered herself hurriedly.

Blake always thought of how fortunate he was to be married to the boss of Mexico's reigning drug cartel, a family who sold tens of thousands of cocaine bricks to drug dealers in seven countries every single day. Losing 12,000 kilos was chump change to the Costilla Cartel.

"Jesus," Alexus said, "we just can't get rid of T-Walk, can we? He's stalking us from the grave."

Enrique nodded and said nothing.

Shaking her head, Alexus said: "I want their heads."

Another nod from Enrique.

She turned to Blake. "Let's get you dressed and on a plane. We're going to The Hamptons, just me, you, and the physical therapists for at least a week at Briar Patch. It's an eleven-acre estate, ten thousand square feet in the main house, four bedroom guest house, sits on a quarter-mile of waterfront. I got it for $140 million last week. There's a gym, you know, so you can get back in shape. It's what you did last time, figured you'd do it again."

This time it was Blake who shook his head; his dick was hard, and he wanted some of his wife's goodies now, not later.

Alexus seemed to read his mind. She raised the corner of her mouth in a half smirk and looked at Enrique. "Hold my mom and the kids downstairs for about thirty minutes. Make sure no one comes in here until then."

Enrique gave an understanding nod and left out, shutting the door behind him.

There were no more words shared between Blake and Alexus. Just carnal moans and groans.

Turns out they didn't even need thirty minutes. He came in twenty.

**Chapter 4

There had been three of them: Fantasia, Jantasia, and Tasia, the three curvaceous yellowbone Olsen sisters from Harlem.

Fantasia was the oldest of the three, a 31-year-old trap queen who'd used the nearly $2 million she made as the sole owner of a well-known Nevada brothel to purchase a string of luxury car dealerships in Chicago, Houston, and Atlanta. She now lived in Decatur, Georgia, in a sprawling hilltop mansion with two black S600 Benzes in the circular driveway, but today she and her 21-year-old sister Tasia were in Chicago, sitting at the back of Great Aunt Micki's, a soul food restaurant on Michigan Avenue.

The middle sister Jantasia — who would be 27 now — had been found murdered in northern Mexico, and Fantasia suspected either Alexus Costilla or Bulletface of her murder. Jantasia and Cereniti, the girl who was found dead with her, had been close friends with Alexus, who happened to own a megamansion just a few miles from where the bodies were discovered in Matamoros, Mexico.

Fantasia and Tasia were here to pay Mercedes Costilla a debt of $120,000 for the 10 kilograms of raw Colombian cocaine she'd fronted them last month and another $120,000 for 10 more kilos. The only reason Fantasia was dealing with a Costilla was to figure out who killed her sister. She had more than enough money; dealing drugs was no longer necessary, though she did occasionally buy kilos for the crew of Bloods her husband ran in Kansas City to sell.

"I don't even like looking at that bitch," Tasia said. "I'm telling you, if this hoe knows anything about Janny getting killed I'm knockin' her ass flat on this floor."

Tasia was young and aggressive, the baddest stripper in the A, in her arrogant opinion, and no one could tell her different. She bit into a piece of fried catfish and chewed.

"Don't go dumb on me, sis," Fantasia chastised. "We can do this the smart way. Let me talk to her. I'll ask all the right questions, she'll open up. It's not like she knows we're Jan's sister. I met her on business. We've hardly even spoken. Right now me and you have the upper hand. Let's keep it that way."

"Don't forget I got that thang in my purse. I'll let her ass have it, on sis. And did you see on TMZ about somebody hacking her sister's phone and releasing a sextape of her and Bulletface?"

"Porsche has a sextape with Bulletface? Wow."

"Fuck Bulletface. I don't give a damn about him, Porsche, Mercedes, or Alexus. If they killed Jan I'm killing them."

"Let me handle this," Fantasia said.

Just then, Mercedes walked into the restaurant with a handsome brown-skinned man and a crew of dark-suited security and headed to Fantasia's table.

"Keep your mouth shut," Fantasia said to her little sister.

Tasia sucked her teeth indignantly and rolled her eyes.

"Heeeey, girl." Fantasia stood up and hugged Mercedes. "Have a seat. I got the bag out in the car."

Mercedes looked distraught. "I can't be long. Got a flight to Barbados. My sister just got shot."

"In Barbados?"

"It's a long story." Mercedes sat down. "Everything with Alexus is a long story. Somebody's always getting killed. Shit's ridiculous."

Tasia cast an accusatory glance at Mercedes. Her eyes flicked over to her older sister and then back to Mercedes.

"Really?" Fantasia said, feigning worry. "I'm here if you need to talk. Let's all just eat and conversate. Talking things out is good for the soul."

**Chapter 5

"I'm Harvey Levin."

"And I'm Charles, welcome to TMZ Live. Today we're starting off with a bang. Grammy award winning rapper Bulletface has reportedly been released from a Miami hospital just minutes after news broke of the sextape of him and Porsche Clark."

"Yes, and according to a news station in Barbados, five men are dead and Porsche was wounded in a shooting that occurred at a restaurant in Holetown, Barbados just over an hour ago. There's no word yet on who the gunmen were or whether or not they were associated with Alexus and Bulletface but many are speculating that it was Bulletface who sent the hit. Blake "Bulletface" King is a reputed member of the Vice Lords, a Chicago street gang..."

Blake aimed the remote at the television and turned it off. They were in an armored black Mercedes Sprinter van — him, Alexus, Enrique, the two therapists, Rita Mae Bishop (Alexus's mother), and his two children, Savaria and King Neal. The kids were asking him a thousand questions; Alexus was scowling at him, obviously still upset over the sextape and his and Lakita "Bubbles" Thomas's relationship; Rita was busy typing on her laptop computer.

As always, Enrique was on his smartphone, managing the Costilla Cartel's daily operations and Alexus's itinerary.

"Daddy," Vari said, "why did you get shot? Was it some bad guys like on the Batman movie?"

Blake chuckled.

"Daddy," King cut in, "My John Cena toy broke and I think Vari did it but she said she didn't but I think she did."

"Boy, ain't nobody broke your toy so stop lying on me."

Blake kept his eyes on Alexus while the kids chattered, and she kept her eyes on him — cold, calculating eyes, the eyes of a ruthless drug cartel boss.

He liked the outfit she'd brought him. True Religion was a favorite designer of his, and black was his favorite color.

"Stop mean-mugging me," he said to her.

She flipped him the middle finger. "Don't talk to me. Talk to them. They miss you; I don't."

Her attitude remained for the rest of the ride to their Palm Island mansion, but Blake didn't care. The pain medicine had him feeling woozy and carefree. All he wanted and needed was a bed and another dose of painkillers to put him to sleep. He would get to see his family and Money Bagz Management recording artists later.

There were five white Rolls Royce's in the driveway of the Palm Island estate, which happened to be next door to Cash Money CEO Bryan "Birdman" Williams' equally luxurious mansion. Palm trees swayed to and fro in the warm breeze.

The first breath of fresh air Blake inhaled as he stepped out of the van was soothing and welcoming. A wheelchair awaited him. Ms. Eden helped him into it and pushed him into the mansion, with Alexus keeping pace next to him.

"Your R&B star wants to leave you for Young Money," Alexus said.

"Who, Mocha?" Blake asked.

"What other R&B star do you have? She's fed up with all the shootings. Wants out. I want the bitch gone, too. I think she likes you a little too much. Knowing you, you've probably already fucked the bitch."

"Ain't nobody fucked that girl."

"Hmm." Alexus gave him the side-eye, and he grinned. "I should push your handicapped ass out of that chair."

He shook his head. "Crazy ass."

"Sure am. You act like it's breaking news."

Her iPhone rang. She answered and put it on speakerphone. Mercedes's voice came through loud and clear.

Loud, clear, and pained.

"I fucking hate you, Alexus."

Alexus gave a half-smirk and hung up without a word. The smartphone rang twice more but she ignored both calls.

"You shouldn't have had Porsche hit up like that," Blake said. "She's family."

"That bitch drugged my husband and recorded herself raping you. She deserves worse, and she's lucky she lived. Bet her trifling ass won't survive the next hit."

In no mood to argue, Blake shut his mouth and eyes and dropped his head back to relax. Already he wanted to get in the studio. He'd grown used to studio sessions over the past few years. With a net worth of $1 billion, he led the Forbes magazine list of the richest rappers, and that number one spot was something he cherished. He knew that rappers like Drake, Lil Wayne, Nicki Minaj, Meek Mill, Rick Ross, and Big Sean were tearing up the Billboard charts, and all he had was five songs in the top 100.

He wanted 100 songs in the top 100. Bulletface was just that ambitious.

"You stress me out way too much, Blake," Alexus said. "Can't believe I had a fucking miscarriage. I wanted another child so bad, and worrying about you killed it."

"Don't blame me for that shit. I was in the hospital. And I'm just as upset, trust me. You know I wanted King and Vari to have a little brother or sister. I'm still sick about losing our baby."

"Fuck you."

Blake shook his head and laughed once. His wife wasn't in the best of moods and he wasn't trying to make it any worse. She preceded them onto the elevator that would take them up to their third-floor bedroom. Blake's eyes fell upon her thick ass. It poked out of her heavy white robe. He would have copped a feel if not for the kids being present.

When they made it to the bedroom, Alexus dismissed the kids. She and Ms. Eden helped him into bed. He immediately grabbed the television remote and went to CNN, knowing that the news of him being released from the hospital would be a top story.

It was, as well as the news of Porsche Clark being shot in Barbados.

Enrique came in and sat down on the arm of an easy chair in the corner. He stared at Blake.

Alexus sat next to Blake and didn't speak until the physical therapists left the room.

"I'll have them and two nurses living in the guest house until your health improves," Alexus said. "Ms. Eden says you'll be ready to hit the gym in a week or so."

Blake shut his eyes. "What's up with Meach and Scrill?"

"They're on tour with Chris Brown and Tyga, I guess. Last I heard, at least. I'm not sure."

"And you sure T-Walk's dead this time?"

Alexus turned to face him and interlaced the fingers of her left hand with those of his right hand. "I'm absolutely sure he's dead. I was there when he was shot. Went to his funeral, too. No more worrying about him."

Blake let out an audible sigh of relief. T-Walk had been his worst enemy. It felt good to have him dead. He couldn't bear another war. Not in the shape he was in. He needed a ton of rest and recuperation. There was no telling how long it would take to get himself back to his old self, and he wanted it to be a peaceful process, not one chock-full of even more shootings.

His body was aching terribly, a direct result of Alexus riding him at the hospital. He didn't want to move, didn't want to think. He just wanted peace.

But Alexus wasn't about to let him off that easily.

"So," she said, planting her hands on her hips as she always did when she was on the verge of snapping, "tell me more about the bitch Lakita...before I send somebody to kill her ass, too."

"You gotta chill, baby. Shit ain't even that deep." Blake closed his eyes, took in a deep breath through his nose, and let it out slowly. "What's wit' those bricks that got stolen? You said T-Walk's people did it?"

Alexus glanced at Enrique, who instantly launched into what had happened and who was responsible.

"Their names are B-Walk and V-Walk. Brian and

Victor, I believe, but they go by B-Walk and V-Walk. They hit our semitrailers before dawn, got the whole shipment fresh out of the submarine."

"You gotta be fuckin' kiddin' me," Blake scoffed.

He couldn't believe it. T-Walk was dead, and still he was a pain in Blake's side.

"Half of that was yours," Alexus said, tracing the bullet scars on the right side of his face with the tip of her pinky fingernail. "Was sending it to your guy Malachi to get off for $26,000 a ki in Chicago and Indianapolis. No worries, though. We have more dope. I just hate that they robbed us. We've got men looking for them now. Cameras on the semitrailers revealed their identities. I don't know what they were doing in Cali in the first place because they both live in New York as far as I know."

Blake shut his eyes and kept them closed for half a minute as he ruminated over the situation at hand. How had T-Walk's family even known about the drug shipment? They must have gotten the information from T-Walk himself before he was murdered last year, Blake decided. Either that or someone close to Alexus and the Costilla Cartel had given them the info.

When he opened his eyes, Alexus was gazing at him with the most loving look on her face. He realized then just how much she loved him, and vice versa. She'd forgiven him every time he fucked up, which was quite often. She'd been there for him through every up and down. He loved her more than he loved himself.

"My cousins," she said, "the ones who were leading that ISIS group in South and Central America. The US-led airstrikes killed all but one of them. That guy who has the same name as my father — my cousin Juan Costilla — is still on the loose, but the entire group of Islamic State militants are believed to be dead now so he can't be much of a threat. He was last seen in Mexico. Got in a shootout with some of our Zeta guys."

"We'll take care of him," Enrique said.

They finished giving Blake the rundown of all that was going on, then Enrique left the room.

Alexus got in bed next to Blake and cuddled up next to him. He shut his eyes again. She lifted his left arm, rested her chin on his chest, and sighed.

He heard the television turn on.

"They're about to be on my ass about Porsche getting shot. Can't believe those ignorant fucks didn't finish her off." Alexus sounded disappointed. She was flipping through TV channels.

"It might be what God wanted," Blake surmised.

He pulled her close and kissed her forehead. "You need to chill the fuck out. Stop acting like Papi."

"Don't you dare bring up my father's name. You're lucky I haven't had you killed for that shit."

He opened his eyes and turned to her, brows furrowed. "For an accident?"

"Fuck you."

"Blame that shit on your sister. She hit me with that bottle, threw my aim off. I was tryna blast that nigga T-Walk."

"Just stop talking about it, Blake."

"Whatever." A small grin shown on his dark brown face. It was a half-grin, on the right half of his mouth because Alexus was on his left and he didn't want to risk being slapped, punched, shot, or all of the above.

The temperature in the black-and-gold Versace-decorated bedroom was a little too warm for comfort. On the wall next to the door was a gold-framed picture of him and Alexus hugged up next to her white Rolls-Royce limousine at the megamansion she inherited from her father's mother in Matamoros, Mexico. They hadn't been there since it was attacked by the same group of Islamic extremists that had ambushed twelve airports across the country and the Minority Television Network tower in downtown Chicago. Seeing the picture brought back a flood of good memories.

He rubbed a hand across Alexus's upper back as she continued to channel surf. Seconds later she paused on an episode of "T.I. and Tiny: The Family Hustle".

"What do you think of us doing a reality show?" Alexus murmured. "Something like, "Bulletface's Road to Recovery". Or "Keeping Up With The Costillas." Something fun, you know. Something people wouldn't mind watching." She giggled softly and kissed his cheek.

Deeming the question far too ludicrous to answer, Blake just shook his head and chuckled once. It was Valentine's Day of 2015, and he couldn't think of a better place to be than right here in Miami with his beautiful wife and family.

Alexus had a habit of sucking on him whenever they were alone. Today was no different.

He checked his smartphone and briefly considered calling Biggs back while Alexus fellated him, but quickly decided against it when her head began bobbing more rapidly. He went to his Soundcloud app and hit play on Dreezy's "Up and Down" as his wife's steadily slurping mouth mimicked the song.

"Happy Valentine's Day to me," he muttered aloud to himself, unaware that this year would be anything but happy.

**Chapter 6

One Month Later...

  Mouths dropped open and eyes went agape when Blake King's pearly white four-door Bugatti Galibier, Enrique's snow-white Rolls-Royce Wraith, and three blacked-out H2 Hummers pulled to a stop in front of Midtown Manhattan's infamous Quad Recording Studios, the place where Tupac was robbed and shot in 1994, and where Bobby Shmurda was arrested in December of last year.

  It was an Empire party— a celebration of Lee Daniels' epic Fox TV series to commemorate the show's season finale— followed by a two-day studio session with Blake's Money Bagz Management recording artists to record their "All We Hear Is Money" mixtape and the last few tracks on his upcoming album, arrogantly titled "The Mansa Musa Project".

  The title was his way of paying homage to the richest person in human history. Mansa Musa had been worth $400 billion; Blake King and his wife's combined net worth amounted to a little over $86 billion, tying them at #1 on Forbes Magazine's list of the world's richest people.

The additional $150 billion in drug money Alexus had stashed all throughout their Malibu mansion raised their fortune to over $236 billion.

Alexus put her hand on the knee of Blake's loose-fitting white Balmain jeans and leaned toward him for a kiss. She wore a skin-tight Dolce & Gabbana mini-dress, all white as usual to display her complete devotion to the color and also to accentuate the white Christian Louboutin heels on her feet, the white croc-skin Birkin bag under her arm, and the gleaming ten-carat white diamonds in her Chanel necklace and Hublot watch. She liked wearing Chanel because of the double-C logo that she used to symbolize her position as boss of the Costilla Cartel, in the same way that Blake rocked Louis Vuitton to symbolize his undying love for the branch of Vice Lords he represented.

Blake was iced out as well, with a white Louis Vuitton skullcap, belt, sunglasses, shirt, bulletproof vest, and duffle bag to go along with his own bevy of blinging white diamonds.

Mercedes and Biggs were in the backseat, equally fresh in all black Versace ensembles.

A phalanx of paparazzi awaited them, but they were respectful and kept their distance as Blake put

on his white leather Pelle coat and stepped out of
the gaudy foreign car. He circled the car to open
Alexus's door, glancing at Enrique and Flako
Costilla — the brother of Alexus and Mercedes's
father — as they got out of the Wraith, and at the
twelve Armani-suited Mexican bodyguards in
trench coats who were exiting the Hummers,
flicking their heads in every direction.

Young Meach, Mocha, and Will Scrill —MBM's
leading recording artists— were waiting in front of
the building with Trav and Ceno of Chicago's
"Sicko Mobb" rap group. Mocha was smiling into a
TMZ camera and talking.

Alexus put on her full-length white mink coat and
joined Blake on the sidewalk.

"Don't say a word," she warned as the paps began
firing off questions.

Blake wanted to check her for even suggesting that
he would talk to the paparazzi. He hardly ever
spoke to the media. He let his music, his money,
and his guns do all the talking.

"Alexus, do you have anything to say about the
shooting investigation that you've been named a
person of interest in?"

"Bulletface, my man, tell us who you believe shot you. Do you think Chief Keef was behind it? Or do you think it was T-Walk again?"

"Kevin Gates said you're his favorite rapper on a recent Instagram video. Have you spoken with him lately?"

"What do you think of Lil Wayne leaving Cash Money and suing them for $51 million?"

Blake kept his lips sealed until they were in the doors and away from the paps.

"Irritating ass paparazzi," he said, leading the way to the elevator.

They all gathered in a large viewing room on the fifth floor. French Montana and Lil Durk were chilling on a semicircular black leather sofa with a few members of their entourages and a dozen beautiful women who looked like urban magazine models and video vixens. Bottles of Ciroc were being passed around. Styrofoam cups of Lean and blunts were in the hands of every man; the women were drinking the vodka.

Blake was anxious to get straight to business with French. There were 500 kilos of pure Colombian cocaine stacked in back of a semitrailer a few blocks down, and French was getting them all for $10,000 apiece.

"Got that sack for you," Blake said, all smiles as he shook hands with French. He saluted Durk, who he knew was a well-known Chiraq savage.

French nodded and went back to sipping his Lean, while Durk began reminiscing with Sicko Mobb about the "Maserati" song they collaborated on a few years ago.

The $5 million French owed was already in the hands of Blake's people and en route to The Versace Mansion in Miami Beach. Blake took a seat next to Alexus and opened his duffle bag. He had his own bottles of Promethazine with Codeine and Sprite soda; all that was missing was ice, which was on the table behind the sofa.

He stacked two Styrofoam cups and poured himself a fill of Lean. Alexus took a rolled cigarillo of Kush out of her purse and fired it up. Biggs began rolling blunts for him and Blake. One of the beautiful models turned on the massive smart TV on the wall across from them just as Empire's season finale started.

"We have to snap some pics for Instagram," Alexus said. "Gotta support my boo Taraji."

"Shhh." Blake reached for the blunt. "Be quiet. Might miss somethin'." The television had his full attention.

Alexus rolled her eyes and sucked her teeth but kept quiet. She was a little upset that her distant cousin Juan Costilla — who had led the ISIS

uprising in Central and South America — was still on the lam from authorities. He was a terrorist like her aunt Jenny had been, and she wanted him dead like Aunt Jenny.

If only she could locate him.

Although Cookie was all she wanted to see, Alexus went to the picture gallery on her iPhone and looked at a photo of her cousin Juan. The photo was taken shortly before his trip to Syria to join the Islamic terrorist organization. He was kneeling on a prayer rug in a mosque, surrounded by other Muslims, and for some reason Alexus found herself wondering who had taken the picture. Maybe it was the wife of his who'd died in last month's US military airstrikes in Puebla, Mexico.

"Man, I would fuck the shit outta Cookie," Blake said suddenly.

Alexus frowned and glowered at the side of his face. His diamond and platinum teeth were shining between a wide smile. She contemplated mushing his face but left it alone and returned her gaze to the TV.

Empire was on.

And she too was a Cookie fan.

It was 9:05 Eastern time.

**Chapter 7

A dark-colored Ford Taurus passed by Quad Recording Studios four times before easing to a stop and parking across the street from Bulletface's sleek white Bugatti.

The big-bellied man in the driver's seat was named Donny. He was a Gangster Disciple from the Englewood neighborhood in Chicago. Shawnna, the girl in the car with him, was from the same block. They had flown in from the Windy City a few hours ago on orders from their gang leader, who'd had a stolen car with two handguns in its trunk waiting for them at JFK.

And now here they were in Midtown Manhattan to carry out a hit. It was in retaliation for the murder of Trintino "T-Walk" Walkson, a multimillionaire TV producer who'd also been a heavily active member of the GDs. Donny had met him once. A lot of the coke and heroin Donny and his younger dealers sold had come from T-Walk. He knew how big of a hit this was just by the amount of cash he and Shawnna would collect for doing it. T-Walk's older brothers were paying them $50,000 apiece for the job, and they'd also receive a kilo of coke to split between the two of them.

"So," Shawnna asked, "are we going in or what? I

can walk in like I need to use the bathroom. Heard that's how Alexus's aunt Jenny was able to kill those people and kidnap Rita at the MTN Tower."

Donny shook his head no. "They'll be out of there sometime soon." He glanced at the time on his phone. "It's a few minutes past nine here. We'll wait."

"Look at those Hummers. I bet they have tighter security than the President. We won't be able to just run up on this nigga. Naw, we gotta catch him at the light and just shoot the whole car up. That's his white Bugatti. Pull down the block and wait."

Donny hated to admit it, but Shawnna was much more intelligent than he. The oversized hoody and sweatpants she wore concealed her slender frame. The big 50-round drum magazine in her 9-millimeter Glock on her lap weighed down so heavily on the sweats that they hugged her thighs. He too wore a black hoody and sweatpants, though his covered a mass of fat. He wasn't ashamed, though. He was a boss. He had six relatively expensive gold chains that he wore daily (though not today), over $120,000 cash stashed in various places on the south side of Chicago, a team of young Gangsters with machine guns for war, and after he killed this young punk he would be $50,000 and a half kilo richer.

He started the raggedy sedan, peeled off in reverse, and whipped around onto 7th Avenue. He parked at the corner. "We can see from here. Don't wanna give em too much of a head start."

"Those Bugatti's go fast," Shawnna said with a laugh. She was gazing out her window at the foreign whip. "Heard they cost about $2 million."

"Fuck dat hoe ass nigga, he got folks wacked," Donny snarled. "He's a opp anyway. Ol' hook ass nigga."

"Didn't say he wasn't. The nigga got money, though. Looong money. Shit, he's richer than Jay Z AND Diddy. Fucked up we gotta smoke his ass."

Shawnna laughed.

Donny grinned and glanced at her thighs. He decided he'd probably get some of Shawnna's goods before robbing her of her half of the reward and killing her.

**Chapter 8

She was like an African American symbol of success, a beautiful strong-black-woman-CEO in an expensive black designer dress.

It was a picture that could have easily been selected for an Ebony magazine cover.

Standing at one of the windows of her 56th floor office at the MTN Tower and staring out over downtown Chicago with tears in her eyes and shame in her heart, Rita Mae Bishop's brain was abuzz with some of the most terrifying memories one can imagine, memories that came from being the ex-wife of Juan "Papi" Costilla, the former boss of Mexico's most deadly and wealthy drug cartel.

She thought of Neal Miller, her last lover, a retired police officer who was shot to death right in front of her last year at the mansion on her private Caribbean island, which she'd named Nevaeh (Heaven spelled backward).

Her own daughter, Alexus Costilla, the new boss of the ruthless Costilla Cartel, had ordered his murder.

She thought of Frederick Douglass, another ex-lover of hers who'd been shot out of the very window that she was now standing at by one of Papi's sister Jennifer Costilla's goons a few years back.

She thought of Nat Turner, yet another of her lovers who'd been murdered by Papi and the notoriously ruthless Costilla Cartel.

And finally she thought of Papi, the father of her only child. Like the others, Papi was also dead. Apparently Blake had accidentally shot him during a fight with T-Walk, the son-in-law Rita had favored.

Another thing that had Rita upset was the memory of being nailed to a cross inside her very own church by the infamous Mexican terrorist Jenny Costilla. It was an indelible memory that she knew would never leave, no matter how hard she tried to forget it.

Her gentle brown eyes refocused on the thick pane of glass, and she remembered Fred making love to her against it mere minutes before his death. Now most of the windows and doors in leading up to her office were bulletproof and electronically lockable. She could fend off attacks simply by pressing a few buttons on her computer keyboard.

With a despondent sigh, she went back to her desk and opened a file on her desktop computer. She was writing a book of short Christian love stories. The idea had come about after watching her own relationships crumble under the evil of the Costilla Cartel. She wanted to show herself and others that happy endings were possible, even if it was pure fiction. As busy as she stayed, the book would take forever to complete, but she was patient.

There certainly wasn't much happiness in Rita Mae Bishop's life, though many assumed that the billions of dollars she'd made with MTN and Costilla Corp. automatically made her the happiest woman on the planet.

The first short story— "Talisha's Tearful Tribulations" — was complete. She was on chapter 2 of "A Thin Line Between Good and Evil", and writer's block had set in days ago. She couldn't for the life of her figure out what to write next.

Luckily, she didn't have to.

Attorney Britney Bostic knocked at the glass door and immediately entered, followed by Dr. Melonie Farr.

"You're late," said Britney.

"Thirty whole minutes late," Farr added.

Rita frowned. "Late? Late for what?"

"Are those tears?" Britney walked around the desk, brows knitted worriedly but wearing the smile she always wore. She was dark and beautiful in a flowing Gucci dress and heels. She hugged Rita. "What's the matter? We're supposed to be downstairs watching Empire."

"Oh." Rita cracked a smile and thumbed away the tears. "Forgot."

"You forgot about Empire?" Dr. Farr asked incredulously.

"Nobody forgets about Empire," Britney said. "Good thing we're recording it. Come on, let's go. We'll watch it at my place."

"No, I'm fine. You two head on out. I'm going home. A lot on my mind tonight. Think I just need some time alone."

"Ha!" Farr shook her head in disagreement. She was pretty in a Rihanna kind of way, only she was nearly as steatopygic as Rita and her daughter. Her shoulderless red D&G dress and custom Giuseppe Zanotti peep-toe pumps accentuated those stunning curves. "You're coming with us, woman. Whether you like it or not," she said in her sternest tone.

Rita gave in quickly. Britney and Melonie were two of her best friends. Though the two were twenty years her junior, they were very mature, strong-spirited, and successful in their chosen careers. Sure, the millions they had in their bank accounts was mostly due to them being lead attorney and therapist to Alexus, but they'd already been success-driven before the Costilla Cartel boss's financial assistance.

With another sigh and a slowly growing smile, Rita got up and went to the coat rack to get her long black mink. She slipped her arms into the sleeves and picked up her black leather Birkin bag.

They chatted about Cookie and Lucious in the elevator, went silent as they made a beeline through the lobby, and in Rita's triple-black Mercedes Sprinter van they discussed Alexus and Blake's relationship while their chauffeur headed off between four blacked out SUVs.

"He'll go back to cheating on her soon," Rita said, holding a crystal glass out to the opening of a bottle of Krug Clos d'Ambonnay 1998 champagne — her favorite, and not just because it was, at $2,000-per-bottle, the world's most expensive 100% Pinot Noir champagne — as Britney filled it to the rim. She sipped a taste. "T-Walk was the man for my baby. I don't know where the idea of loving that criminal she's married to now came from, but she should have made a better decision. He's so unbelievably hard-headed. He's a thug, like Tupac or something. I don't like it."

"Join the club," Britney said. "Not a lot of people like that Alexus and Blake are together, but what do you expect? This isn't the good old days. Bad guys today are real bad guys. They have to be. Look at the way our young black men are being killed all across this country. They're killing each other, police are killing them. There isn't much hope. They have to be tough guys like Blake if they're from the ghettos of America, because it's the only thing people in those communities respect."

Melonie shook her head. "They can leave and make something of themselves."

"Yeah, but what do they do until that opportunity is presented?" Britney countered. Now she was filling Melonie's glass. "What if they never get that opportunity? Or better yet, what if they are trying to do good and succeed in school, but the guys on the street they live on are at war with a rival gang who drives by every day or so in hopes of catching anyone they can catch, because one of their own gang members has been slain? Bullets don't discriminate." She turned to Rita. "I know you're big on putting everything in God's hands but no amount of prayers will stop the killings. Gang culture is a part of America that'll never change. Blake has adapted to that fact and made himself heartless. Gotta respect him for that."

Rita shook her head and drank her champagne. Personally, she believed God was in control of everything, but she never pushed her ideologies onto others. If Britney didn't believe in God's power and glory then that was on her.

"Whatever the case," Rita said. "Blake's a billionaire. He shouldn't be living like a thug. That's why Papi didn't like him."

"Money can't change a person if they don't want to change. Blake's a gangster at heart." Britney set the bottle down and stretched out her legs.

The Sprinter was spacious and comfortable, with heated white leather seats, a glass-doored refrigerator full of the Krug champagne and 24-carat gold bottles of "Acqua di Cristallo Tributo a Modigliani" water ($60,000 per 750 ml bottle). There were laptop computers on the mahogany tables in front of the seats and three smart TVs over the large, darkly tinted windows. The storage compartment under the van opened from both sides and held two dozen suitcases and bags that belonged solely to Rita and Alexus.

Rita took a long moment to ponder over her son-in-law; then, "I just hope he can keep himself out of trouble this go around. I don't think his body can take another bullet."

"Twenty-one he's taken so far." Britney went from scrolling on the laptop to suddenly slamming it shut. "I can't take it. Everybody on Facebook, Twitter, and IG is talking about Empire. And we're missing it!"

Rita and Melonie cracked up laughing.

"Settle down." Rita reached for the remote control that was laying next to her laptop, turned on the TVs, and went straight to Fox 32.

It was only 8:08 Central time.

They glued their eyes to the televisions, and Rita upped the volume until Cookie's voice was loud and clear.

**Chapter 9

"Man, I ain't watchin' this gay ass shit!" Blake snapped suddenly as the two men he was watching on the wide-screen began a passionate kiss.

He hopped up and grabbed Alexus by the wrist, flicking his eyes around for the restroom. There was one at the rear of the room but he wanted more privacy, so he headed out into the hallway and located another restroom down the hall. Alexus's heels clicked and clacked across the clean marble floor.

"I see that limp's leaving." Alexus snickered happily, but Blake didn't look at her until they were in the restroom.

He locked the door and pushed her up against it.

Her mouth was an alluring spread of dazzling white teeth and red-painted lips. He mashed his lips onto her bottom lip and sucked on it, while his hands lifted, dropped, and squeezed her plentiful backside through the snugness of her dress.

She lifted his shirt and clawed at the Teflon vest beneath it. Then her fingers were struggling with the gold LV buckle on his belt, unzipping and unfastening the baggy Balmain jeans. She yanked out his lengthy love muscle and stroked it in both hands as their tongues danced.

She pulled back from the kiss, cheesing and shaking her head. "Wonder if Tupac or Biggie ever got some pussy in this restroom."

"Bulletface gon' get some for em," Blake said, grinning his signature diamond grin and thumbing the dress up to her waist.

"Is that so?"

"Yup."

"I should've divorced you when you fucked that stripper bitch. If she was here you'd probably stick your dick in her."

"Stop bringing up old shit."

"You're lucky I'm addicted to you."

"Shut that shit up."

Blake lifted her legs up onto his waist and then slipped his twelve-inch member deep into Alexus's tight, lubricious pussy.

She sucked in a breath. Her hands went to the sides of his neck, and again they kissed as he started slamming in and out of her juiciness.

They bumped and grinded against the door for a long while. Then Alexus dropped her feet to the floor and turned her back to him. She looked over her shoulder at him, biting the corner of her lip and fixing her long, curly black hair in a ponytail.

Blake slapped his length across her ample cheeks before guiding it back into her. He studied his own reflection in the sink mirror as he started thrusting forth and back, his strong black hands gripping her narrow waist, his pole fully impaling her every time he thrust forward.

"Shiiiiiiiiiiiiiit," Alexus said, stretching out the word as Blake stretched her insides.

He settled into a quick-paced rhythm and made her moan like crazy for about twenty full minutes.

Someone knocked on the bathroom door and opened it just as Blake was spurting his seed into his billionaire wife.

It was a young black girl in a hoody.

"Oh, my God!" she said, eyes wide. "It's really you. Bulletface. And Alexus. Wow."

Blake's brows knitted. He put his dick away with semen still dripping from its head and zipped up his jeans. Alexus hurriedly fixed her dress.

"Sorry you had to see that," Alexus said with an embarrassed giggle.

"I just, um...need to use the toilet. Sorry," said the girl in the hoody.

Blake gave her a wary stare and noticed that there was something heavy and big in the double-ended pocket of her hoody as she disappeared into the first of three stalls.

He reached for the .45-caliber Ruger pistol in the Louis Vuitton holster under his left arm and nudged Alexus toward the door. She got the hint, reached in her Birkin, and pulled her gold-plated .50-caliber Desert Eagle halfway out of the bag as she exited the restroom ahead of Blake.

Quickly, he yanked her to the side of the door and waited.

She laughed. "All those shots you've taken might have you a little too cautious, Blake. That girl ain't—"

The restroom door swung open.

The barrel of a gun became visible first, then the hands of the girl in the hoody on the gun's handle.

In one swift motion, Blake grabbed the girl's pistol in his left hand and swung the butt of his own gun at her jaw with the other.

He knocked her out cold.

**Chapter 10

"Bitch need to hurry the fuck up. Don't take that long to piss."

Donny was nodding his head ever so slightly to a Jim Jones club banger. The back of his head was relaxing on the threadbare headrest. His thumbs were drumming on the steering wheel. He was cold, and the heat didn't work.

His mind was swarming with thoughts of him burying his face in Shawnna's pussy. That would get him warm. He'd tongue-punch her clitoris to the beat of this bullshit Dipset song.

"I bet that's all they play in New York," he muttered aloud to himself. "Nothin' but Jim Jones and Busta Rhymes. And DMX." He laughed at his dull joke and considered opening his eyes to see if Shawnna was on her way back from the restroom, but he hadn't slept much last night, and the big meal he'd eaten at his and Shawnna's hotel room had him feeling too sleepy.

The passenger door squeaked open a minute later. He didn't bother opening his eyes just yet. A few more seconds of rest was all he'd need.

"Took you long enough," he mumbled.

"Who the fuck are you?"

The strong male voice startled Donny. His eyes shot open, and he reached for the gun in his hoody.

The Hispanic man in the passenger seat had a gun with a silencer on it aimed at Donny's face, and for an instant Donny thought it was jammed. He thought he'd be able to reach his gun and kill the evil-looking man.

He saw the first flash, and he never thought again.

**Chapter 11

When Shawnna Jackson came to she was lying on her side in the trunk of a car that wasn't moving.

Was it parked?

Was she about to be dragged out of the trunk, shot dead, and thrown in some dumpster to rot until her body was found, if it was ever found at all?

She trembled in fear.

Her hands were tied behind her back. Her ankles were roped together. The right side of her face was throbbing painfully. There was tape on her mouth.

She tried with all her strength to free her hands but it was no use.

Fuck, Donny. Where the fuck are you? she thought.

The sudden sound of the trunk popping open frightened Shawnna.

She squeezed her eyes shut and didn't move. Playing dead was better than being dead.

Somebody grabbed a handful of her hair and used it to pull her out of the trunk. The pain of her hair nearly being yanked from her scalp ended the fake dead play; she squinted through the pain and groaned.

The next thing she knew, she was being dragged

away from the car (a sparkling white Rolls-Royce) and through the snow leading up to the front door of the largest home she'd ever seen.

The man doing the dragging was an angry Mexican in an expensive black suit.

**Chapter 12

Enrique threw the girl who'd worn the hoody (now she wore only a purple bra and black panties) into the fireplace and began dousing her head and body with lighter fluid.

They were in The Hamptons, in the opulent living room of Briar Patch, the most expensive home on the East Coast.

Seated on the sofa next to Alexus, puffing on a blunt and sipping from his Styrofoam, Blake watched the terrifying scene unfold before him; Alexus, seemingly unbothered by it all, was tending to her fingers with a nail file.

"You really don't know who you're fucking with," Alexus said, . "Neither does your boss, whoever he or she is. I'm the boss of all bosses. You're breaking the chain of command even attempting to come after me. Tell me who sent you on this foolish little mission and you might live. Don't tell me and...well, you know. You don't. You don't live to see another day. We wouldn't want that to happen."

Enrique ripped the tape off the girl's mouth.

"B-Walk sent us," the girl said quickly. "He sent me and Donny to kill Bulletface. It's all because of what happened to T-Walk. Please don't kill me, I got a four-year-old son—"

"Oh, shut up. Tell me where to find T-Walk's brothers and you'll live."

"I don't know. I heard they stayed somewhere in Indianapolis. Or they might be in Michigan City, where T-Walk was from. That's all I know. Just ask Donny. I left him in the car. He might—"

"We found Donny," Alexus said.

"He's no longer with us," Enrique said. He lifted an iron poker from beside the fireplace and struck the girl on top of her head with it.

Blood spurted from her scalp. She started screaming: "HELP! SOMEBODY HELP!"

Alexus drew the .50-caliber from her bag and aimed it at the girl's face. "Shut up or die. Your choice. I don't wanna hear all that screaming now. You weren't screaming when you walked in that restroom."

But the girl would not stop screaming.

Alexus got up and crossed the room to the fireplace, screwing a sound suppressor into the weighty handgun's triangular tip. She put the silencer's barrel against the girl's forehead and pulled the trigger twice.

The girl who'd worn the hoody lost the back of her head and all of her brains. Then Enrique took Alexus's gold Zippo lighter and set fire to the brainless corpse.

**Chapter 13

The stench of the dead girl's burning body drove Blake out of the room. Suddenly the Lean in his cup wasn't so appealing. He went outside to his Bugatti and set the cup down on the trunk. Alexus was at his side a moment later.

"That bitch deserved it," she murmured, snuggling up to him and resting her chin on his left shoulder. "I don't know what the hell T-Walk's family has in mind but they've got us fucked up. I'll have every single one of them killed."

Blake shook his head in disbelief, and Alexus continued her furious rant.

"First they jacked us for twelve thousand bricks, and now they wanna send these fucking rookies at us. This is the kind of shit that makes my blood boil. I can't wait to find those assholes. I took it easy on their brother; I won't be so kind with them."

"We need to find them as soon as possible," Blake said finally.

"They disappeared without a trace after their guys hit our trucks. Enrique said fifteen of the kilos from that shipment were found in an Indianapolis drug bust two weeks ago. Other than what that girl just told us that's all we've got."

Blake pressed his palms on the cold trunk and

leaned forward, thinking. He knew he had to get to the remaining Walkson brothers before they got to him. In the past he'd been shot twice as many times as 50 Cent and then some, and he wasn't about to let it happen again. No, from here on out he would plan every move, as if life itself was a chess game.

No stalemates.

No losses.

Only checkmates.

The new, wiser philosophy prompted his decision.

"Tell them to get our bags to the jet. We're moving to Indianapolis for a week or two. On vacation, you know." He turned around and put his hands on Alexus's hips. She immediately took advantage of the moment to peck her lips against his. "We'll be back to business in no time. I wanna make my presence known out there, though. Somebody'll tell me somethin'," he said.

Just then, Mercedes— who'd been in an upstairs bedroom with Biggs— came storming out the front door of the mansion, wearing a black robe and furry black slippers and looking like she'd just woken up.

"What the fuck, Alexus?! Why is there a dead body burning in the fireplace?!"

"Just be happy it's not your sister," Alexus retorted snidely.

Porsche had yet to return from Barbados. Blake believed that Porsche's prolonged vacation had a lot to do with her fear of Alexus and the Costilla Cartel.

With a last disdainful look, Mercedes sucked her teeth and disappeared back into the mansion.

***Chapter 14

Porsche Clark was not in Barbados as her sister Mercedes was making everyone believe.

In fact, hardly anyone she'd known before the shooting knew of her whereabouts now.

Sure, she had lived a flashy lifestyle around Alexus and Mercedes, and in some ways she still did. Only difference is now she wasn't riding around Chicago showing it off as she'd done in the past.

She had a new boyfriend who had once lived in the Parkway Gardens apartments on 64th and Calumet Avenue. He was a Black Disciple nicknamed Glo, a tall, heavy-set man with tattoos covering his whole upper body, including his face. A high-ranking BD and close associate of GBE and OTF, he was respected all throughout the Englewood neighborhood. When Porsche met him he had just bought a long black Escalade ESV; she, on the other hand, had just recently broken up with Hot Rod and sold the black Bentley coupe he'd bought her and the pink Bentley that Alexus had bought for her a few years ago.

She and Glo were living in a four bedroom home on 64th and Eberhart that she had secretly purchased for $127,000 shortly after they moved in. Glo was under the impression that they were paying rent. He knew that she was related to someone who was related to Alexus Costilla. He also knew that she had more cash in the bank than the measly $22,000 she had in the account they shared, because last week when she'd "put a down payment" on the beet-red 2015 Range Rover she now had parked out front behind his Escalade, the money in their account had still been there.

Porsche actually had over $741,000 in one personal account and exactly $500,000 in another, but that was between her and her accountant. She was keeping Glo out of her business. She had taken a liking to him after literally bumping into him backstage at a Lil Durk show in Milwaukee, but to her he was nothing more than a real nigga with some good dick. With the way so many young guys were running around Englewood killing each other, she didn't know how long she had before Glo joined the cemetery gang, and she wasn't about to be the fool and blow all of her money on him just to have him lose it all in one spray of bullets.

She did however spend freely on things for the house...and on bricks of cocaine that she often bought from her sister for less than $10,000-a-kilo.

This morning she came in the back door carrying five large shopping bags and a gallon jug of milk. She had on black leggings, a shirt, and Gucci heels because Glo loved it when she wore leggings and heels.

Glo was standing at the refrigerator with the door open, looking around inside it. On the kitchen table behind him was a Glock pistol with a 30-round extended clip in it and another extended clip lying next to it.

In this treacherous neighborhood full of Black Disciples, Gangster Disciples, Mickey Cobras, and Vice Lords, "No Lacking" was the motto. Getting caught without your strap was practically suicide.

Glo looked at her and then at the milk.

"My nigga," he said, suddenly smiling as he grabbed a box of Frosted Flakes off the top of the refrigerator and an enormous bowl out of a cabinet.

Shaking her head and smirking, Porsche took the bags to their bedroom and returned to the kitchen.

"Those people from Vivid called again," Glo said.

Vivid Entertainment had made several offers to Porsche for the rights to the sextape she'd made with Blake, but she wasn't interested. Not after she'd nearly been killed in Barbados because of it.

"Next time tell them to stop calling our house," she said, holding her hips.

"You need to quit playin' with them people and take that money."

"And get killed? No thank you."

"Them niggas ain't gon kill shit."

"You don't know Alexus like I know Alexus. That bitch is crazy and so is her family."

"I'm just trying to understand how we're living on

the south side of Chicago when you know the richest person in the goddamn world. That's all I wanna know. Evidently you ain't doing something right."

Porsche rolled her eyes. "Glo, it ain't as simple as it seems. Trust me."

"All I trust is a bankroll," Glo said, stuffing a large spoonful of cereal in his mouth.

"You need to start trusting yourself to shop instead eating every damn thing I go out and buy." Porsche leaned a shoulder against the stainless steel fridge and stared at her brawny man. He was shirtless with a pair of sagging gray Coogi sweatpants and Jordan's of the same color. "We'd really be straight if you just listened to me and got your guys together to make one major move against Blake and Alexus. I'm telling you, I know where to hit them. My sister set up a lick for T-Walk's brothers that got them over ten thousand kilos. We can hit do better than that. We can hit Blake where it hurts."

Glo crunched his way through a mouthful of Flakes; then, "How we gon do that?"

"I've already told you. Get all the BD's together and have them record a video demanding that Blake and the rest of MBM start paying your gang every time they perform in your city. Hell, get the GD's to do it, too. He's always talking that gang shit. Well, make his ass start paying. Bulletface loves Chicago. He wouldn't know how to respond to something like that. He wouldn't have any choice but to pay up. As long as you put the message out and make it so he has to talk to you before he can perform, you'll get the money. Have the younger BD's start shutting down every MBM show that comes to the city. Trust me, he'll pay up, of only to keep his other artists out of the drama. You'll be able to milk him for at least a few million."

Glo nodded. "Sound good."

"Because it is," Porsche said.

"A'ight, I'll holla at the folks. We gon demonstrate that thought. I really need a good reason to do somethin' like this but I'll figure it out."

"A good reason? Wasn't Blake into it with GBE last year? Is that not a good enough reason?"

"Yeah...yeah, folks n'em will go hard about that."

"Well, use that excuse. Or just say he needs to start paying y'all for even doing shows in your city. Whatever you need to do to get in his pockets, do that shit. If you gotta have some niggas shoot up one of his shows then so be it. Whatever it takes. I'll even—"

Just then, seven gunshots rang out.

It sounded like they were coming from somewhere in the alley out back.

Dropping to the floor, Porsche muttered, "If they put one hole in my Range..."

Glo was as fearless as they came. He picked up his gun and went to the back door. "Stay down," he said, glancing back at Porsche. "Matter fact, get in the room."

But Porsche got right up and followed him as he opened the door.

There was a teenaged boy on the ground next to the rear left tire of Porsche's Range Rover. He was gasping for breath, and there were three small bleeding holes in his T-shirt.

Two more teens—one in a black jacket, the other in a green hoody, both with shoulder-length dreadlocks and guns with clips that were as long as Glo's — were running up on the wounded kid with their pistols aimed at him.

Porsche knew both of the gunmen. They were young Black Disciples who were sometimes seen with the guys Glo hung around.

She assumed the wounded boy was a Gangster Disciple.

"Drag his ass across the alley first!" Porsche ordered. "Y'all ain't about to make our house no crime scene!"

"Move!" Glo barked as he grabbed the wounded boy's short dreads and threw him to the other side of the alley.

The boy hit the door of the garage across the alleyway with a heavy thud.

Then the two gunmen got right up on him, aiming at his face, and shot him multiple times. Glo shoved them into the backseat of his Escalade, blew

Porsche a kiss, and then sped off up the alley, quickly getting the two young drillers away from the grisly murder scene.

 Porsche sat on the back porch when the police arrived and taped off the alley, smoking cigarettes and drinking beers out of Glo's cooler full of Miller Genuine Drafts. (He liked the beer mostly because he said MGD stood for "Murder GD's").

They asked questions. Had she seen anything. Had she ever seen the young man in the neighborhood. Did she know his name. No, no, and no, she said. She didn't know a thing. Saying anything else, she knew, could easily lead to her being the next unsolved murder of the year.

Other neighbors were out watching the flashing blue and red lights and the sheet-cloaked body in complete silence. Like Porsche, they knew nothing, though they probably knew everything.

Sasha, the 16-year-old daughter of Porsche's nosey neighbors Eric and Deidra, ran over to Porsche just as the dead body was being loaded into a van. The teenager was so busy typing messages on her smartphone that she almost tripped on the first stair. She wore snug-fitting black jeans and a matching hoody with OTF stretched across the chest in gray and blue letters. The lettering went along well with her black, gray, and blue Air Forces and the sparkly blue gloss on her lips.

"Hey, P," Sasha said in a rushed tone. "My momma wanna know if she can get a cigarette until she get her check in the mornin'. She said she'll give you three back if she can get two 'cause my daddy need one, too."

Porsche's first instinct was to say, "No." Just as she'd done with the police. But she liked Sasha's and had been waiting to show the young girl that she was just three years older and just as cool, so she gave in and told the teen to follow her inside.

"That is so messed up what happened to Gerome," Sasha said as they passed through the kitchen. "He went to my school and everything. You know that's Larry Hoover's cousin, right?"

"I don't know anything about anybody in this area. I'm from out west." Porsche picked up her pack of Newport's from the coffee table in the living room. She realized then that the pack was empty and looked at the young girl, wondering if she was looking at a virgin or local thot. "And I don't know that boy, either. Really don't care to know him. His ass must've been with that BDK movement. That's the kinda shit that happens to brick niggas like him."

"You a BD?" Sasha asked, leaning on the dark leather couch. Her mother was light-skinned and her father was coal-black; she was a balanced brown, with the hips and breasts of a grown woman.

"Nah," Porsche said. "My man is. Where I'm from

out west, ain't nothing but 4 Corner Hustlers,
Stones, and Vice Lords. You smoke? I'm all out but
I'm heading back to the store to get me another pack
now."

"You can't tell my daddy, but yeah I smoke. My
momma knows. She smokes em wit' me. I know I'm
young but I be needing cigarettes. My last two
boyfriends got killed back to back; my cousin
Johnny just got killed on O Block, and my brother
Steve got shot, too. I might go crazy if I don't
smoke." Sasha sat on the arm of the couch,
simultaneously texting on the phone and cracking
what seemed to be every knuckle in her fingers.
Seconds later she set the phone on her lap and
looked up at Porsche. "How did you get that red
Range Rover? My daddy said that must've cost you
a lot of money."

Porsche replied with a smirk.

"Did you really fuck Bulletface?" Sasha asked. "I
saw it on TMZ and Media Takeout. They got still
images. I wanna know if it's a real sextape or just
some pictures, and if it is real— you know— how
was it. I mean, who doesn't wanna know?
Everybody at my school is talkin' about that
sextape. In the one picture it looks reeeaal big. Like
my arm." She laughed and held up her arm.

"Ask your momma if you can go to the store with
me. I'll get her a pack of cigarettes, and she won't
owe me nothin'," Porsche said.

There was something about Sasha that Porsche truly liked— well, actually there was a lot she liked. She liked Sasha's womanly curves. She liked Sasha's pretty lips.

Though she hated the realization, she wanted to kiss those pretty lips.

She grabbed her Gucci purse off the table and gazed fixedly at Sasha's plump backside as the sexy young girl walked out the back door and shouted Porsche's message to Deidra, who immediately agreed to let Sasha go after warning her to stay safe. "I'm safe as can be," Sasha said when they got in the Range Rover. She reached a hand in her hoody's belly pocket and pulled out a bulky chrome revolver to show Porsche. "Momma bought me this .44 Bulldog when Steve got shot up. I know how to use it too, so if a opp hoe pull it just get back 'cause I'm blowin'."

Porsche was all smiles as she pulled off in her SUV, though the police cars parked all along the alleyway had her a little nervous to be in the car work two handguns (hers, a 9 millimeter Glock, was in her purse).

"I'm planning on making some million-dollar moves real soon," she said to Sasha. "You can be a part of it if you wanna."

Sasha's eyes flicked over to Porsche, and for a moment she said nothing.

"What kinda moves?" she said finally.

"Major moves. Boss shit. I'm talking nothing less than a million dollars right off top. Might have to fuck over one of your favorite rappers to get it, but it's worth it."

"Fuck a favorite rapper," Sasha said. "Them niggas ain't putting no money in my pocket."

Porsche smiled and high-fived Sasha. "That's my girl."

*Chapter 15

38th Street in Indianapolis is the strip where all the hood guys and girls came to show off their best outfits and big-rimmed cars and trucks, the place where dope boys from all over the city came to put on for their hoods and occasionally catch up with their rivals. Gunplay and brawls were commonplace. If you had a baby-mama in Nap town during the summer months, she was likely to be found somewhere on "Trey-Eight" on most nights with a crew of her friends, most of them scantily clad in revealing skirts and shorts and searching for an even bigger baller to skeet a child support check in them.

But this was the middle of March. Snow was falling. Most of the girls were packed into cars with their friends, or gathered inside restaurants and other businesses along the busy strip.

Brian "B-Walk" and Victor "V-Walk" Walkson weren't from Nap. They were rich young niggas from Michigan City, Indiana. The nearly $20 million their baby brother T-Walk left to them in his will made the Walkson brothers the richest street niggas in Indianapolis, and the 12,000 kilos of raw cocaine they'd hit the Costilla Cartel for last month had them on top of the dope game.

Cruising the strip in his burnt orange Hummer H2 on matching 34-inch Forgiato rims, B-Walk was chain-smoking blunts of Kush with V-Walk, who was two years his senior. B-Walk had a pile of hundred-dollar bills on his lap that amounted to over $100,000.

V-Walk had an equal amount of cash in his right hand and an iPhone 6 Plus in the other. He was texting Spradley— the biggest drug-dealer they'd met in the city thus far— to see if he was ready to shop with them again. Last month Spradley had bought 250 kilos for $3 million cash; the Walkson brothers were hoping to see at least another $3 million tonight.

"He better shop before we go back to Chicago," B-Walk said. "I ain't comin' back out here until the summer."

"Yeah muhfuckin right, nigga. If he come with them M's we slidin' out here asap."

B-Walk chuckled. His brother had a point. There was no way they were going to neglect one of their biggest spenders.

A chameleon-painted Suburban on 30's with "Haughville Deuce" airbrushed across its rear window whipped in front of the Hummer and honked.

"Look at this nigga," B-Walk said.

"You know him?" V-Walk asked.

"Hell no."

"Pull up next to him. See what he talkin' 'bout."

B-Walk veered around to the side of the Suburban and rolled down his window.

The Suburban was full of women, young black girls with squinted eyes and wide smiles. They were bouncing around to the sound of a Bulletface song that was banging from the speakers in back of the Suburban.

The driver— a cute-faced redbone— said, "Hey, boy. Where y'all from?"

"Not Nap," B-Walk said.

"And definitely not Haughville," V-Walk added, leaning toward the driver's side to get a closer look at the girls. He caught a glimpse of an attractive girl behind the driver. "Where y'all headed? And turn that wack ass Bulletface off."

"Nigga," the driver said, turning the music down, "Bulletface is that nigga. You wish you had his money."

Though even the slightest mention of the man they suspected of having their brother murdered infuriated the Walkson brothers, they managed to keep their cool with the girls.

"We finna hit my girl Kierra's party at Pure Passion. I'm lookin' for some work, too."

"How much?" B-Walk asked, suddenly enthused.

"A half a thang, nigga. You ain't got it. Pull over right here at the Subway on Grand."

B-Walk didn't hesitate to pull over behind the Suburban.

He was his father's only dark-skinned child. T-

Walk had been as light-skinned as V-Walk. They'd already sold 495 kilos— 250 of them for $12,000 apiece to Spradley, 50 to Baby Mike from 42nd and Post Road for $16,500 each, and 175 of them had gone to a faction of the Gangster Disciples in Chicago they were closely tied to for $10,000-a-ki. The remaining 20 bricks had been broken down and sold to low-level dealers the brothers knew in Champagne and Chicago in Illinois and Indianapolis, Gary, South Bend, Anderson, Muncie, Michigan City, East Chicago, Hammond, and Fort Wayne in Indiana. With well over $5.5 million in cash made in the past month alone, they felt obligated to spend a hundred grand or so every night they went out in what had come to be known as "Dub City"; as long as they made some money in the process.

B-Walk pulled up alongside the Suburban and gawked at the driver's incredible body. He knew she would look a million times better standing.

"I'm Bria," she said. "You probably know my baby-daddy TJ, the one who got popped off the other day in that drug bust out west."

B-Walk didn't know TJ, but he guessed Bria's "baby-daddy" was an associate of Carl, a dope boy from Haughville who Baby Mike had served after shopping with B-Walk. Baby Mike had called with the news that a nigga he'd served had just gotten raided the day after he bought the fifty kilos. Then Brian and Vic had seen it for themselves on the news.

"You mean the nigga who got jammed up wit' Carl?" B-Walk asked.

"Yeah, that was my baby-daddy," Bria said.

They exchanged numbers and Bria agreed to follow Brian to the liquor store on 38th and Sherman and then to Pure Passion, the number-one strip club out east.

At the liquor store, Brian bought 10 fifths of Hennessey, 5 fifths of Remy Martin, a few cases of Pepsi and Sprite sodas, and two gallons of orange juice for the afterparty they would have. He saw the hungry looks on the girls' faces as they eyed his bankroll at the counter, but he was mainly focused on Bria. She was short and thick in all the right places, small-waisted, pretty-faced, and bow-legged. 'FREE TJ' was stretched across the chest of her sweatshirt. Her ass was enormous in her snug blue jeans.

B-Walk was all smiles.

As they left out, Bria leaned in close to him and said, "Boy, I'm gon' fuck the shit outta you tonight."

"At the club? In the truck? Lemme know where, shit, we can do that now."

"Nuh uh, I ain't no thot," she said with a laugh.

He got back in the H2, staring at Bria's generous curves as she hopped up into the Suburban, and headed down 38th feeling like a street king. He had the baddest bitches in every city vying for his attention, and all he did was fuck them once or twice and move on to the next one.

His phone rang, and he answered it as soon as he saw the caller's photo pop up.

It was a call from the girl who'd set up the Costilla Cartel robbery for him.

Her name was Mercedes Costilla.

**Chapter 16

Costilla Corp. owned seven private jets, fourteen luxury helicopters, and five Boeing 767s, two of which Alexus used to transport her and Blake's fleet of armored vehicles wherever they travelled.

By 7:00 am, they were at JFK airport on Alexus's private jet, and once the vehicles were loaded on the 767s, Enrique — a registered pilot since 2007 — took to the sky.

Blake sat silently across the table from Alexus, promoting his artists' latest albums and mixtapes to his 49.1 million Twitter followers and 42.8 million Instagram followers. The Honduran mahogany table in front of him was piled high with the $500,000 in hundreds he'd had in his duffle bag.

Across the aisle, Mercedes was pouting, arms folded on her chest, eyes cast out the oval-shaped window. Blake couldn't understand why she was pouting, but he didn't care enough to ask. She'd already tried setting him up to get killed by T-Walk once before, and no matter how much she apologized he knew he would never trust nor have love for her again.

Biggs was sipping Lean and writing music on his smartphone, his hearing blocked out by an iced-out pair of Beats headphones.

Two flight attendants emerged from the kitchen

with breakfast: Scrambled and boiled eggs; steak;
turkey bacon; pancakes with blueberries,
strawberries, and bananas; and shrimp and grits.

A text message from Alexus popped up on Blake's
phone just as he started eating:

'Idk wtf is up with Mercedes. I still don't trust that
hoe bae'

Blake replied: 'U know I don't either'

'At least T-Walk's gone. We know she can't be
working with him lol.'

'What about his brothers? Think she know them??'

'Don't think so. I never even met them'

'Yeah, u would know. Hot ass.'

Alexus kicked at his leg under the table and
squinted at him; he chuckled and went to his camera
to snap a photo of her over the mountain of cash.

"I don't know why I hang with you people,"
Mercedes said suddenly; she hadn't talked all
morning.

Alexus frowned. "The fuck is that supposed to
mean? Because last I checked these 'people' made
you a fucking millionaire."

"Fuck that money. My whole family's dead
because of you and Blake. And what's a few million
to a bitch like you? You owe me way more than
you've given me."

"I don't owe you shit."

"Yes the fuck you do!" Mercedes snapped. "You owe me big time. You would have life in prison if I told the cops who was behind the Whitney murders. You'd get life for a lot of shit."

Alexus didn't get a chance to reply.

"Bitch!" Blake said, the right side of his upper lip rising in a savage scowl. "I wish you would snitch. Ol' rat ass bitch. Kinda shit you on? Don't get fucked up on this plane. Throw yo' ass out that door wit' no parachute."

Mercedes jumped up and grabbed her hips, looking to Biggs to stick up for her, but he kept right on vibing to whatever beat he was listening to.

"You know what, Blake?" Mercedes said angrily. "I got a cake baked for yo' punk ass, nigga. And you ain't gon' see it comin'."

"Shut the fuck up." Blake wasn't about to argue with his wife's sister. He went back to business on his iPhone.

But Alexus was far from done.

"I'll tell you what," she said. "As soon as this plane lands in Indianapolis, you can take your ass to Barbados with that shiesty ass sister of yours. Me and you might have the same daddy but I don't know you from a can of paint. You're from grimey ass Chicago and I'm from hustling ass Texas. Bitch. I'm Alexus motherfucking Costilla. If you don't wanna be around me then leave. Won't bother me none."

"Keep on pressing my buttons, Alexus. Keep on and see what happens."

"Bitch—" Mercedes lunged at Alexus without another word.

Alexus came up swinging and landed a flurry of punches to Mercedes's face. Mercedes fought back, but missed with every blow.

Then Blake's fist crashed into the side of Mercedes's head.

She hit the floor and didn't move. Alexus kicked her in the face twice.

"Stupid ass bitch!" Alexus shouted.

Biggs threw off his headphones and stood up. His eyes went from Mercedes to Alexus and finally to Blake.

"Damn, what the fuck, bruh?" he said, picking Mercedes's unconscious body up from the polished wood floor and setting her in her seat.

"When we get to Nap that bitch gotta go," Blake said, gritting his teeth. He hated disrespecting the man who'd saved his life during the Miami shooting, but Mercedes had crossed the line going after Alexus.

Biggs carried Mercedes off to the restroom. Blake heard the door shut and lock.

"If that bitch comes out of that bathroom on

bullshit I'm killing her ass," Alexus said, kicking off her heels.

"Sit down, baby. We only got a half hour till we land. We shouldn't have been lettin' that snake ass bitch live wit' us anyway."

"I know." Tears of anger filled Alexus's eyes. "I only do it because Papi asked me to. Those were his last words. He said, 'No snitching...and take care of Mercedes.' That's the only fucking reason I take care of that bitch."

"Sometimes you gotta make your own decisions. Parents ain't always right." Blake hugged her tight against his chest and kissed her forehead. "Fuck what Papi said. Listen to me. I'm your husband, and I say fuck that bitch."

**Chapter 17

Biggs sat Mercedes on the 24-karat gold toilet seat, splashed some water on her face, and gave her a few slaps, but it still took her a couple of minutes to come to and several more seconds to figure out where she was.

"What…happened?" she asked.

"You okay, baby?"

"Mmm."

"Just relax. You got a knot on the side of your head and a swollen lip but that's about it. You should be good."

Mercedes leaned forward, put her elbows on her knees, and dropped her face into the palms of her hands. Biggs rubbed her back.

"How did she knock me out?"

"Don't even think about it, baby. Here." He filled a small cup with sink water and offered it to her.

She took a small sip. "I'm killing that bitch."

"You can't be serious," Biggs said, lifting her chin with the side of an index finger. "Alexus is a billionaire. She's the richest muhfucka on the planet. Chill the fuck out and enjoy that shit. Look at how much money we got. I just bought my momma not one but two houses off the money I got from Blake. Why the fuck you can't just lay back and eat?"

She pushed his hand away and dropped her head. "I lost my kids fucking with these people. I lost my momma and my kids, and now my sister is scared to come and see me because of how scared she is of these goddamn Mexicans. And don't let me get on Blake."

"Ain't nothin' wrong with Blake. He's a real street nigga like me. Ain't never snitched on no nigga, ain't never backed down, always about that bankroll. You're just mad at him about that old shit. You need to apologize to them for that stunt you just pulled."

"Apologize?!" Mercedes was incredulous. She lifted her head and tried to stand, but a spell of dizziness sent her back to sitting on the toilet seat.

"Relax, baby," Biggs said.

"Oh, I'll relax alright. I'll relax when we get to Nap. And Blake's punk ass will, too. You can believe that."

**Chapter 18

'...targeted airstrikes against Islamic extremists in southern Mexico have erased the threat the terrorist group posed to the United States, but according to the FBI, Juan Costilla, the most dangerous terrorist of the group, may have escaped to northern Mexico and crossed over into Texas. Here is a photo of what the FBI says he might look like today...'

"I think I know that guy," Juan said, standing shirtless at the television with a cup of Starbucks coffee in his hand.

Juan had done what his great aunt Jenny did to get into the country— after dying his hair blond and undergoing numerous facial reconstructive surgeries, he'd used a Sinaloa cartel drug tunnel to enter the States with a new identity. Now he was Alberto Martinez. Jenny had plugged him with a Sinaloa cartel underboss who wasn't much feeling Alexus Costilla's new role as boss of all the drug cartels. His name was Manuel, and he'd gladly allowed Juan guarded access to the tunnel and even threw in a box of handguns, $25,000 cash, and a waiting limousine ride to the opulent Four Seasons Hotel in Chicago.

That had been two days ago.

Today Juan was still in the same $399-a-night executive suite. Maryann, the blonde-haired teenaged prostitute lying naked across the bed, was snorting a line of coke off the case of the Taylor Swift album she'd taken out of her purse last night. She was a stunning young white girl from Missouri with a beach body, an alcoholic mother, and a father she hardly knew.

"There's no way you can know that guy," Maryann said. "He's one of those no-good pig-hating terrorists. Probably cut off your head for nothing."

"You think?"

"Of course he would. He's the guy who was beheading journalists and aid workers in those ISIS videos. One of those piece of shit Muslims. My mom says they are only proof that the world is coming to an end. When you have people supposedly worshipping God but killing thousands of innocent people in His name, it's pretty much a sure sign, you know. I'd never even give a Muslim a handy-J, no matter how much he offered to pay. I hope they all burn in hell."

Juan sat down next to the girl and caressed her lower back while she snorted up another line.

"Have you heard of Alexus Costilla?" he asked. "Or Bulletface, that, uhh...rapper. The guy Alexus Costilla's married to."

Maryann looked back at him. "Come on now, Alberto. Everybody knows Alexus Costilla. She's the queen of the world, for Pete's sake. More famous and rich than Paris Hilton, my idol. God, what I'd give to be her. I wouldn't want the big butt but I'd certainly like the money."

"Know where I can meet her?"

She looked at him again. He smiled.

"What?" he said.

"Just wondering why you want to meet Alexus. You aren't one of those crazy fuckers, are you?" She gave a nervous laugh.

"I hear cocaine makes you paranoid," Juan said.

"Very funny." She didn't laugh. "I'm not sure of how someone could go about meeting Alexus. I know she owns The Versace Mansion in Miami Beach. You might be able to find her there, but she's probably always on a private jet somewhere."

"I need to find her. There's five grand in it for you if you can help," Juan said, still rubbing the pretty girl's back.

"Just check her Instagram. You'll see where she's at on there. She's always posting pics with Bulletface." She got on her smartphone. Seconds later she said, "Indianapolis. She just posted a pic from the airport in Indianapolis. Look."

Juan grabbed the phone and looked at the picture. In it Blake King was sitting in a Louis Vuitton leather seat on what looked like a private jet. The table in front of him was piled high with cash. The caption beneath the picture read: #NapTownBound #CircleCity

A diabolical smile spread across Juan's face.

"How long does it take to drive there?" he asked.

"A few hours. Not long."

"Well," he said, getting up and putting on his black silk shirt, "let's get going."

**Chapter 19

"Stop posting on Instagram so muhfuckin much," Blake said.

"Boy, bye. I posted one picture. That's what IG is for."

"You know I don't like that shit."

The sound of the bathroom door opening silenced them.

Blake and Alexus kept an eye on Mercedes as she returned to her seat with Biggs.

"I'm sorry, Lex," Mercedes said.

Alexus wasn't trying to hear it. "Fuck that. When we get to Nap you can leave. I can't be around a bitch I can't trust. I give you the world and you don't appreciate the shit. Fuck you."

"I know. I'm sorry."

"Sorry doesn't cut it. You're always accusing me of being bad for you, so now we'll see how you do on your own. Good luck."

"She can stay," Blake said, but it was only because he liked having Biggs around. Biggs had grown on him over the past few months. He'd already given Biggs a shout-out on a song off his upcoming album, and every celebrity in the music industry was used to seeing Biggs with him at strip clubs and industry parties.

Alexus didn't say another word to her sister. Minutes after the plane landed she and Blake were in the backseat of his Bugatti Galibier and on their way to the Indianapolis Marriott East hotel. Biggs and Mercedes were in one of the SUVs with the bodyguards.

Alexus took a mirror and a stick of MAC lip gloss out of her bag and applied some to her lips.

"Think I should kill that bitch?" She said it as if her sister was nothing more than a bothersome bug that needed to be squashed.

"I don't know." Blake was pouring some Promethazine with Codeine into his Sprite-filled Styrofoam. "She ain't really a threat as long as she's around us. Might wanna get her phones tapped, though. She threatened me. Said she got somethin' planned."

"That's why I should just kill the bitch."

Blake laughed and leaned toward his wife. He kissed her on the cheek. "Knew I married you for a reason."

"You're not the only crazy nigga in this relationship. Don't forget who my father was. I'm just as deadly."

"Stop it," Blake scoffed. "You ain't nowhere near as fucked up in the head as Papi was. I still remember when he cut off that girl's head and put it in my car in Mexico."

"Don't forget her tits, too."

Blake laughed. Alexus laughed. In the driver's seat, Enrique laughed.

"That nigga was fried." Blake turned to his window and stared out at the passing traffic as Enrique drove down 38th Street.

All the cars, trucks, and SUVs on shiny chrome rims were captivating.

"These Nap niggas put rims on everything," he muttered, more to himself than to Alexus.

"When I was about sixteen," she said, "Aunt Jenny brought me here for the Circle City Classic. Oh, my God, you should have seen it. It was as if Rides had shipped in every car they ever featured in their magazine. I came to the Indianapolis Black Expo that year too and it was the same way. It's what they do here, I guess. I like it."

"Yeah, me too."

Blake got on his iPhone and checked the notifications bar. The first thing he noticed was an Instagram notification from a girl named BaddieBarbie1. He tapped on the Instagram app instead of going to the message and saw that the girl had commented on a number of his photos.

Judging from her profile picture, she was an eye-catching dime piece.

He wanted to go to her page for a closer

examination but Alexus was too close for comfort so he went to one of the comments the girl had left:

'When is ur next tour??!! I LOVE U, Bulletface!! Come to Atlanta!! I'll be front row at Young Meach's show tonight!! Pleeeease notice me!!!!'

He grinned and went to the next comment she'd left on a photo of him backstage at an MBM concert with Young Meach, Will Scrill, and Mocha:

'If you ever come to Club Onyx in Atlanta ask for Baddie Barbie!! I'll give you lap dances alllllll night long!!!! Lol Bulletface marry me pleeeeeeease!'

So, she a stripper, he thought. He shook his head and decided to chance a quick glance at her page.

The first thing he noticed was that she had over 250,000 followers.

The next thing he noticed was just how unbelievably beautiful and curvaceous she was in the most recent photo she'd posted. She was lying on her stomach in a large bed, wearing a pair of black boy shorts and a small T-shirt and counting through a stack of hundreds.

Reluctantly, he double-tapped the photo, and left Instagram for his email before Alexus could catch him in the act.

****Chapter 20

"I need a favor. A huge favor. Promise I'll pay you back as soon as I get my baby daddy outta jail and make this first flip."

Here we go, B-Walk thought as he sat up in bed and looked down at Bria. He knew some money would come into play sooner or later. Especially since she'd sucked his dick and let him fuck her from the moment they had entered the hotel room until they both were too tired to keep going..

"What kinda favor?" he asked.

"Ten bands. To bond my baby daddy out, that's it."

"What happened to you wanting to buy that half a brick?"

She giggled and dug her hand into the front of his boxers. "I was just saying that to see if you was really ballin' like I thought you was. I wish I could buy a half a thang. TJ got popped off with everything. I told his dumb ass to have a stash house, but noooo, his smart ass wanted to keep everything at his sister's house. Feds got all that shit. All I was able to keep was the truck, and now he's trying to get me to sell that for bond money. His bond is $200,000, pay ten percent, you know. His grandparents gon' put up the other half."

"Why the fuck would I wanna help you bond that nigga out when I know he ain't gon' do nothin' but keep you away from me? In this situation I'm better off not helping."

She pulled out his love muscle and kissed it on the head. "That nigga ain't gon' stop me from doing me. We ain't even together. He just takes care of our daughter. That's the only reason I want him out."

"I'll think about it."

"You better do more than think."

"You better do more than kiss," he shot back.

The side of Bria's lovely brown face rose to a half smile. She sucked the head of his dick into her mouth and began stroking its length in both hands.

B-Walk pushed his boxers down and enjoyed the energetic blowjob she gave him. They had retired to the hotel room at around 2:30 in the morning and they'd fucked and sucked each other senseless until sleep took them. V-Walk was in the adjoining suite with two of Bria's friends.

Giving Bria the $10,000 was no big deal to B-Walk, but he wasn't sure if he would. He wasn't big on giving his money to women. His mother and his kid's mother were usually the only exceptions to the rule, but since the both of them were currently vacationing in Turks and Caicos with way more than enough cash to hold them over for years to come, he figured it wouldn't hurt to help Bria out a little. Maybe she'd suck his dick like this every day he was in town. And besides, he needed something to do until Spradley came to re-up.

Then maybe he'd find that fuck-nigga Bulletface and avenge his baby brother's death.

Flicking his eyes around the luxury hotel suite, he thought of Donny and Shawnna, the Chicagoans he'd sent to go after Bulletface in New York. He wondered why he hadn't yet heard back from them.

But then he said fuck it and just enjoyed the tight, warm feel of Bria's mouth as he lay in bed in his favorite hotel in the city— the Indianapolis Marriott East.

**Chapter 21

'I'm bout dat murda game like Boosie

Cop Bugattis like hoopties

Young Bulletface, trunk full o' K's

Keep choppas on me like groupies

R.I.P. to A$AP Yamz, shouts out to Rocky, my nigga

I'm still poppin' zanz and sippin' Lean, till I'm in the sky high witcha

Got Louis all on my belt, Balmains all on my waist

Birds all on my scale, and B's all in my safe

So fuck yo M's nigga I'm too paid

Like Sosa daughter I got 2 K's

And I'm too cold nigga, snowflake

No I can't go nigga, no way

My bad bitch off Kush and drank

Her money fill the whole bank

She love it when I pull out the sword

And stab her wit it, O.J.

These fuck niggas stay hatin' on us

Who gives a fuck, okay

Cause when I up the yoppa on a opp or coppa, I guarantee I'm gon spray...'

"Now," Alexus said, smiling from ear to ear, "that's my boo right there! That's the old Bulletface that made you a platinum-selling rap artist! Shit, spit that again!"

Blake gave an indifferent shrug, but inside he was just as hyped up about the verse he'd just recorded on his Ipad. He couldn't spit it again even if he wanted to. He had freestyled the entire verse. He'd have to listen to it a few times to memorize it.

They were pulling up to City Dump Records, an Indianapolis recording studio that Blake had used a couple of times before. He hadn't felt like going to the hotel just yet. It was much too early, plus he was in town to find T-Walk's brothers, and he knew that he wouldn't likely find them at a hotel.

He was here at the studio to meet up with Baby Mike, a rowdy young Vice Lord he'd served a few times in the past. Baby Mike was recording a song with some of his hood guys.

Mercedes was already at the hotel, and now Biggs was in the passenger seat beside Enrique, toking on a blunt of Blue Dream Kush. He passed it over his shoulder to Alexus.

"Is that him?" Biggs asked as a short, chubby light-skinned man in a red leather Pelle jacket came walking out of the building.

"Yep," Blake said, but he made no move to open

his door.

The Bugatti was bulletproof, safe for all who remained inside it.

He lowered Alexus's window a little, and Baby Mike reached in for a handshake.

"What's up, lord?" Baby Mike said. "The fuck you doin' out here, nigga? Heard you was recuperatin' from that hot shit."

"I'm good now," Blake said. "Out here lookin' for T-Walk's people. I heard they want a word with me."

"Aw, shit, them niggas out here. I don't know where they stayin'. I got the nigga B-Walk number. Why, he on some bullshit? 'Cause I'll have my lil niggas ride down on him asap. You awready know, bro, we straight thang out this way. Niggas blowin' hellie straps. I done shopped wit' the nigga before but it's whatever, bro. Gimme da word and I got his ass today, my nigga. On Vice Lord."

Blake grinned. Maybe he wouldn't have to be in Nap town for as long as he'd thought.

He leaned closer to Baby Mike and lowered his voice, though he trusted everyone in the car to keep their lips sealed. "I ain't never offered a nigga no shit like this, but I got a whole shipment for you. Sixteen thousand bricks. You get both of them in a morgue as soon as possible and I gotchoo."

The look on Baby Mike's face was priceless. His eyes widened with his mouth. He drew back and looked around the parking lot, then moved back to the window.

"Bro! Sixteen thousand?" he said in utter disbelief.

"Yeah. I gotchoo, bruh. Just get that shit handled and hit me when it's over. I need that done immediately."

"Bro, on my dead niggas I'm on it. Say no more."

Blake nodded his head and gave Enrique a tap on the shoulder.

The shiny white Bugatti slipped out of the parking lot and into the Howard Street traffic.

**Chapter 22

Rita's mouth spread into a glorious smile when she spotted her two grandchildren running toward her through O'Hare International airport ahead of Justine, their nanny, and a slew of Mexican bodyguards.

She was standing near the escalators with Britney. The sight of so many bodyguards looming over Vari and King was disheartening, and Rita might have voiced her opinion if not for the massive influx of fans that kept walking up asking for selfies with the number-one talk show host in America.

She kept a kind disposition throughout the impromptu photo shoot and left out of the airport holding King's hand and listening to him tell of a great movie he'd watched on the flight.

"...And then the man with the hammer, um, he beat up everybody with the hammer, when it flew out the sky, and it hit the ground but they couldn't get it out the ground because, um, they wasn't strong like the hammer man—"

"It's called Thor, you big dummy," Vari said.

King frowned discontentedly. "Hey, I'm not a big dummy."

"Well," Vari said, "little dummy. I stand corrected."

The snide remark elicited a burst of laughter from Rita and Britney.

King Neal didn't find it funny. He pouted and crossed his arms.

"She's only kidding, King," Britney said, and gave him a pat on the shoulder. "Vari, don't call your brother names."

In the Sprinter, Rita said to Britney, "I don't like this life for my grandbabies. It's great being wealthy and all, but it's too much for these kids to be going through. Their father's a gangster, and their mother is a —"

Britney raised a silencing index finger. "Not in front of them." She canted her head toward the kids.

Rita didn't like being silenced but she knew that Britney was right. Vari and King had already been through hell and back being raised around a Mexican drug cartel and a world-renowned gangster rapper. They didn't need to know all the details of their parents' criminal activities. Not at this age, anyway. But there would definitely be a time when Rita would tell them if their parents didn't. They had to know the truth one day.

As if on cue, Rita's smartphone rang at that very moment with a call from Flako Costilla, Alexus's uncle and the underboss of the Costilla Cartel.

She ignored the call.

"Who was that?" Britney asked.

"Flako. You know I don't like talking to that man. Never have. An argument with him is what led to me meeting Papi in the first place."

"Isn't that a good thing?"

"I suppose so. But only because of Alexus. Aside from that I wish I'd never met either of them. They're all a bunch of lunatics." She flipped open her laptop and changed the subject. "How were last night's ratings for the BHJP finale?"

BHJP was Brick House of Jupiter Island, a reality show on the Minority Television Network that was now the second most-watched show on primetime TV (next to Empire, of course). Brick House of Palm Beach was also a hit show.

"Twelve million viewers last night. Just five behind the Empire finale," Britney said. "The girls are asking for a quarter million per sode next season, and Thunder says she's leaving because she feels like somebody in the Costilla family might have been behind T-Walk's murder."

"Thunder can't leave. She's our biggest star."

"That's what I said."

"Offer her more money." Rita became thoughtful. She bit her thumbnail. "We can't let her go. That would destroy our ratings. Another network will grab her right up."

"I'll handle it." Britney typed on her own laptop for a few seconds. "The girl Shanni fought at that hair salon on last week's episode has filed a lawsuit

against MTN and Costilla Corp. She's seeking
$750,000."

"Let her sue. She won't win a dime."

"Okay, and Diddy wants MTN and MTN Sports to
start running primetime commercials for Revolt,
Ciroc, and Sean Jean. Two years for $2.4 million."

Rita shrugged. "Sure, why not."

More typing. Britney's slender black fingers
moved hurriedly across the keyboard. She was all
business in a powder blue Prada pantsuit and
Manolo Blahnic flats. The flawless diamond ring on
her left hand symbolized her marriage to Shannon
Manning, though now they were separated due to

him having gotten another woman pregnant.

Again Rita's smartphone rang, but this time it was
Alexus calling on Facetime.

"Hey, old lady," Alexus said with a beaming
smile.

Rita wasn't smiling. "You really should stop
leaving my grandbabies alone while you and Blake
are out traveling the world."

"Oh, please. They're perfectly fine with Justine."

"That's what you thought before King was
kidnapped by those men in downtown Chicago. It's
not like you have a lot to do. I manage everything
for you. The least you can do is watch your own
kids."

Alexus rolled her eyes. "Can I see them? Or is that

too much to ask?"

"Don't you ever roll your eyes at me," Rita chastised. "Have you forgotten whose mother I am? Last I checked I had a daughter named Alexus Costilla. Don't make me go upside your head, Ms. Thing. You're not too old to get whooped. And ask your uncle why is he calling me. You both know that I don't like being involved with that side of things."

"Okay, Ma. The kids?"

Shaking her head and seriously considering socking Alexus one good time, Rita handed the iPhone to King and then went back to her laptop.

The little guy was talking to his parents when a dark blue Ford sedan drove up alongside the Sprinter as it was stopping at a red light.

Rita immediately noticed that the two white men in the car had on sunglasses, and for some reason this made her uncomfortable.

"Look," she said to Britney, and nodded at the Ford. "I may not be the brightest Harvard graduate in Chicago, but something tells me those men are watching us."

"That's Sneed, isn't it?"

They both knew FBI Special Agent Josh Sneed. He'd been in charge of watching Alexus numerous times before.

Upon closer inspection, Rita came to the conclusion that it was indeed Josh Sneed.

But why was he following them?

She wondered if Flako's call had anything to do with it.

**Chapter 23

"Okay, I love you, daddy," Vari said, and Blake hung up.

He turned to toss the iPhone back to Alexus, but she was too busy sitting at her throne getting her hair, fingernails, and toenails done at the same time, so he set it down beside him on the bed and looked at his beautiful wife.

She was in a black leather swivel chair in front of a mirror in their hotel suite at the Indianapolis Marriott East. Enrique was napping in an easy chair in the corner nearest Blake; the other bodyguards were standing around doing nothing and making $100-an-hour.

"I'm going to the club tonight, Blake. Me and that snake-ass sister of mine," Alexus said to his reflection. "I'll get her in line. I don't know what in God's name has gotten into her but I'll fix that shit tonight. Let's just hope your friends get that other problem taken care of as well. I don't want any loose ends."

"Shit, you think I do?"

"No, I'm just saying. We've been having problems stacked on top of problems over the past few years. It'd be nice to have things go smoothly for once."

"Everything'll work out. Don't even worry, baby. I got it."

Blake went back to scrolling through beats on his Ipad. He put his diamond-encrusted headphones on so that one speaker was sealed around his left ear and the other was on the right side of his forehead.

"How much longer before you have that album done?" Alexus asked.

Blake shrugged.

"Who's all going to be featured on it?"

"I ain't figured that out yet, but so far it's just me. Now will you shut the fuck up and let me work?"

"Can't that wait until you get to the studio? We're here because of you — the least you could do is spend some time with your wife."

He shook his head and pulled the other speaker down over his right ear.

Alexus flipped him a middle finger.

He grinned and chuckled and went back to listening to his beats.

A Kanye West beat caught his ear and he quickly thought up a hook. As usual, he began recording a freestyle verse on the Ipad that would later be rerecorded in his studio.

'Welcome to I.N.D.I.A.N.A. where Ignorant Niggas Die, It's A Nasty Atmosphere, a scary place to ride

Welcome to Indiana, (jeah)

Welcome to Indiana, (jeah)

Welcome to Indiana, (jeah)

Welcome to Indiana

Blakey from Michigan City

Where niggas don't shed tears, they get em tatted on em

Run up wit semis murkin every nigga dat ratted on em

Well at least that's what I'ma do

They hit Meach wit da hammer too

Fore you reach I'ma blam the tool

Grit my teeth when I hammer dude

He shot me...he gon see what da mini Mac'll do

I'm hungry, so I'm turnin' his skinny back to food

Back back I'm boutta act a fool

Backpack full o' supplies, I'm lookin' like I'm goin' back to school

From M City, I was born real

So come through, if you think Indiana just full o' cornfields

That's a good way to getcha squad killed

Walk over dem tracks, see how long it'll take fore you getcha orange peeled

It's simple as that, click-clack it and clap

Ya spinal cord'll shift in ya back, get hit for ya stacks (jeah)

Get resolved if you problematic, revolvers and automatics

When I'm done blastin' you better call on the paramedics

You tough bastards'll get it faster, I'll wreak some havoc

Have you chumps askin' why niggas leave the scene in a casket

So start actin', and you'll lose ya face

And I be movin' weight at a grueling pace in the Hoosier state

You dudes is cakes, in the holster is where da Ruger stay

I keep it for you fakes but it's mostly for niggas who da states

You conversate wit da jakes, that'll getchoo erased

Young goons skippin' school, now we see higher truant rates

We blowin' loud and takin' Remy to the face

Whole hood caught cases, I'm happy my nigga Tooter straight

These no-good Caucasians, they just sit and wait

For the dough we make from the shit we be
scrapin' off the plate

Before they come and watch and start runnin' in
our doors

I was facin' 65 and they wanted to gimme more

And my hoes wanted to take me home like Remy
Ma

Man I'ma stop, ain't no need to spit any more...'

Alexus was staring at Blake with her mouth wide
open. So was Jeanene, the stunningly beautiful
black Floridian woman who was doing her hair, and
Enrique, who was suddenly awake and on his feet.

Moved by their undivided attention, Blake decided
to go for another verse.

'Look, I was thinkin' of stoppin', but I ain't finna do
it, It would be a sin to do it

Rap game platinum, you see how easily I'm
spinnin' through it?

You talk smack, you'll getcha team wacked

Guns stuck to dey necks like nicotine patches

Yeah, I'm the Midwest king of dis rap shit

Seen wit' da team, blowin' green like it's Patrick's

Stash in the same ol' springs in the mattress

And guns like the ones wit Marines in Iraq spit

You wanna run off in my stash cause you needy

I'll clap and throw da hun'eds on ya back, rain meezy

When shit get sticky da clips get empty

And like a minute man I'ma bust this quickly

Lace y'all's kicks, better run 'fore I lace ya

Mac 10 shells give you thugs motivation

Slugs from the K blow the mugs from ya faces

Them cases is nothin', my dawgs on vacation... Welcome to Indiana...'

Content with what he'd recorded, Blake pushed the headphones down around his neck

"Babyyyyy!" Alexus shouted.

"See," said the hairdresser, "that right there is why people love you so fucking much. Did you just freestyle that song?"

"He always freestyles," Alexus told her. "In my opinion, he's better at it than any other rapper, and I'm not just saying that because we're married."

"Wow," Enrique said, nodding his head thoughtfully. "You've got some raw talent, Blake. Seriously. That has to be the reason you've survived all those shootings. God can't let you go just yet. Not until you've gotten a lot more of that hot stuff released."

"Thanks, y'all." Blake stood up and stretched. He

contemplated heading down the hall to Biggs and Mercedes's room but quickly decided against it when he thought of the vicious punch he'd given Mercedes on the jet.

Instead of leaving the room, he picked up his smartphone and called Biggs.

Gunfire erupted just seconds later.

**Chapter 24

"How many bullets are in that thing?" Mercedes asked, referring to the large drum magazine in the gun on her boyfriend's lap.

"Fifty," he said.

"Jesus Christ. What can you possibly need that many bullets for?"

"A fuck nigga."

"I'd put fifty in Blake's punk ass."

"No the fuck you won't," Biggs grumbled.

"Why are you taking up for him? You're supposed to side with your woman. A real man sides with his woman."

"I'm supposed to side with my brothers."

Mercedes sucked her teeth, and a cantankerous expression darkened her face. She was holding an ice pack to the knot on the back of her head and watching Biggs devour a lunch of crab cakes and pasta at the glass kitchen table.

The smartphone on his hip started ringing at the same time that someone knocked at the door of their hotel suite.

Mercedes immediately regretted telling B-Walk her room number. She hoped it wasn't him knocking.

Frowning, Biggs pushed away from the table and got up, curling his mighty brown fingers around the handle of his Glock 17. He checked his phone. "Aw, it's Blake," he said, walking to the door.

Mercedes held her breath.

Unlocking the door, still chewing a bite of pasta, Biggs glanced back at her, and again he frowned.

"What?" she said.

He opened the door.

Mercedes gasped.

Victor "V-Walk" Walkson was standing at the door with a slim dark-skinned girl who looked to be hardly a few days over eighteen.

"Is Mercedes here?" V-Walk asked, eyeing the gun Biggs was holding. "She knows me. Tell her it's V-Walk."

Biggs instantly raised his gun, but V-Walk pushed the girl in front of him and drew his own pistol just as Biggs started pulling the trigger and backpedaling, crouching low and moving toward Mercedes.

The girl caught three bullets to the front of her left shoulder and two more to the back of her skull, the fateful result of being sandwiched between the two incessantly barking handguns.

She hit the floor with gaping holes in her face.

Biggs tried his best to hit V-Walk somewhere in

the upper body or head as the man scrambled to his left and dove out of sight.

"Don't run after him!" Mercedes shouted, grabbing Biggs by the arm. "Stop shooting!"

Biggs shifted his eyes to Mercedes and regarded her with a frigid scowl.

He swung the gun quickly, catching her high in the temple; she yelped in pain and dropped to the gray marble floor.

"Bitch, you tryna set us up?!"

"No, baby! I called them Blake!"

Biggs had the growing inclination to put a hole similar to the ones in the other girl's face in Mercedes's forehead.

He aimed his gun at her and put his finger over the trigger.

"You tried to set my nigga up," he said, his tone replete with anger and disbelief.

Just as he was about to pull the trigger, Alexus, Blake, Enrique, and a dozen more bodyguards appeared in the doorway.

When he looked up at them, Alexus and her men all had their guns trained on him. Blake was holding his LV duffle, eyes wide as he studied the dead girl's body.

"Don't you fucking dare," Alexus said. "I can't stand the bitch myself, but I'll be damned if I let you kill my sister."

"This bitch tried to set us up," Biggs said, looking at Blake. "The nigga V-Walk just came to the door...for her!" He jabbed the smoking barrel into Mercedes's forehead.

Blake frowned up immediately and drew his gold-plated .50-caliber Desert Eagle — identical to the one Alexus was pointing at Biggs— from inside his duffle bag.

Unsure of how Blake was feeling, Biggs almost took aim at the Money Bagz Management CEO.

**Chapter 25

"Everybody hold up," Blake snapped, and aimed his gun at Mercedes. "You had one of them niggas come here? So you really was plottin' on me, huh?"

"They were already here!" Mercedes cried.

Blake saw red. He was about to do what he'd been wanting to do for a long while now. He'd never trusted Mercedes. He'd wanted her dead ever since the day she had set him up in Miami.

He applied some pressure to the trigger, already envisioning the sight of Mercedes's brains all over the floor next to her...until Alexus turned her gun on him.

His anger faded into an expression of incredulity. He lowered his gun, grabbed the barrel of Alexus's, and pressed it against the center of his forehead.

"You want me dead, too!" he growled.

"Don't do this, Blake. Papi told me to watch after her. She's my only sister."

Blake noticed that Alexus hadn't taken her finger off the trigger.

He pushed her gun aside and waved for Biggs. "Grab yo' bags, bruh. Let's slide. We might catch them niggas leavin'."

Alexus's men kept their guns on Biggs until he and Blake were in the elevator. Blake saw tears in Alexus's eyes, and seeing them broke his heart more than the fact that she'd pulled a gun on him.

But the fact that she was taking her snake-ass sister's side over his outweighed the love he had for her.

He watched her until the elevator doors closed, pushing to the back of his mind the reality of what he knew was imminent.

He was about to leave his wife, and with the way he was feeling about the Walkson family, he doubted if he'd ever return.

****Chapter 26

As Blake was racing away from the hotel in his Bugatti, his phone started ringing nonstop. The calls were from Alexus and Enrique. He ignored them all and slowed down as police cars zoomed past in the opposite direction.

"Fuck them hoes, bruh," he said.

"On Vice Lord," Biggs agreed. "Fuck em. That was some foul shit. She could've got us both wacked."

"Wish you would've shot that bitch before we walked in."

"I was just about to pop her muhfuckin ass, too. God was on her side. Had to be."

Blake was grateful for the dark tint on his windows; driving down 21st Street, he spotted several pedestrians recording footage and taking pictures of his shiny white Bugatti as he passed by.

At a red light, he checked his phone and saw that Enrique had sent a text letting him know that they had the hotel camera recordings in their possession. There would be no surveillance evidence.

Alexus had also text messaged him, but he didn't bother reading it.

He told Biggs about Enrique's text.

"I didn't kill that bitch anyway," was Biggs's hasty reply. "That nigga V-Walk shot her in the head. Twice. I was tryna get him."

"What was he wearing?"

"Hell-if-I-know. A white T, I think. I know he was high yellow, like T-Walk was."

Blake gritted his diamond and platinum teeth as he stopped at yet another red light.

A chameleon-painted Chevy Suburban swerved around his car and shot through the red light, barely missing another SUV that was crossing the road at the same time.

The Suburban's luck ran out at the next red light.

It crashed into the rear driver's side of a red Toyota and sent the little car spinning around in the middle of the street. The Suburban stopped...but only for a few seconds. Then it took off again.

Blake's eyelids became stringent slits. Biggs looked equally perplexed.

"What the fuck...?" said Biggs.

With a thoughtful nod, Blake took off after the Suburban.

**Chapter 27

"Bruh, I might be wanted for murder," V-Walk said as soon as his brother answered the phone.

"Murder? Damn, nigga, I just left yo' ass thirty minutes ago and you done offed a muhfucka?"

"It was that bitch Mercedes. I came to her room and some nigga opened the door. Soon's I said my name he upped strap on me."

"Where you at?"

"On my way out west with Bria. Her lil buddy Kierra got killed in the shootout, and her dumb ass crashed into somebody's car as soon as she sped off from the hotel. She tried to stop but I was like fuck that. We on our way to her spot in Haughville. Hurry up, bruh. Come pick me up."

"I'm on my way."

Brian had his Hummer parked near the entrance of Sutton Place apartments right off 42nd and Post Road.

He was here to meet up with Baby Mike, who had called about an hour ago saying he was in need of another fifty kilos.

"Shit," B-Walk said.

Just then, Baby Mike's canary yellow old-school Delta 88 on white 28-inch floaters pulled up beside the Hummer and stopped.

The call from Vic had B-Walk paranoid. He reached under his seat for the .357 Magnum he kept there and set it on his lap.

Baby Mike's passenger window rolled down.

"Sup, bro?" Baby Mike said. He had on an all-black Coogi outfit, which on a normal day would not have raised any red flags.

But Vic's situation had Brian on high alert.

"Not shit. We gotta hurry up. Gotta go scoop my big bro in a minute."

Baby Mike smiled. "Aw, shit, it ain't gon' take that long. Here, I got somethin' else for you, too." He leaned over and opened the glove compartment.

B-Walk lifted the .357 an inch off his lap, and when he saw the gun Baby Mike was pulling out of the glove compartment, he opened fire.

Baby Mike's brains were evicted without notice a second later.

Heart pounding with adrenaline and fear, B-Walk stomped on the gas pedal and fled the area, rolling high above all the other cars and trucks on his 34-inch rims.

**Chapter 28

The Suburban finally came to a stop at a one-story home on the corner of Medford Avenue and 12th Street. Judging from the murals on several cars, a bunch of graffiti, and the words on the sweatshirts and jackets of a crew of dope boys on the street, this was the Haughville neighborhood.

Blake pulled over and parked one block down. He had the bulky Desert Eagle on his lap. A double Styrofoam of Lean was in his left hand, along with a blunt that was wedged between his index and middle fingers.

"Last time I came here," Blake said, picking up and cradling the golden gun in the palm of his right hand, "I laid some niggas down about my daughter. A bitch ass nigga named Lil Matt that my baby mama was fuckin'. The nigga was one of them down-low fags, Vari caught him fuckin' a punk who stayed next door. We came out here and shot the whole block up."

"Fuck all that talkin'. What we on?"

Blake had to smile. Biggs was ready for some action.

"Hold on. Just watch for a minute," Blake said, looking at the Suburban as three of its doors swung open.

Two girls and a light-skinned man in a sky blue

jacket leapt out of the SUV and jogged up the stairs of the house they'd parked in front of.

"That's him, bruh," Biggs said, and pushed open his door.

Shaking his head, Blake grabbed ahold of Biggs's arm. "Hold on, Lord. We ain't gotta put in no work. That's what we got money for."

"Man, fuck that! These niggas sent some muhfuckas way out to New York to get at you, bruh. I wish Lil Lord was out to see this shit. He would've murked everybody."

"Well, he ain't here. Close that door. Let me call my nigga Baby Mike. He'll send a nigga over here to take care of this clown."

Biggs slammed the door shut. His reluctance was palpable. He stared straight ahead, while Blake dialed Baby Mike's number.

After getting no answer, Blake took a Mac-11 submachine gun out of his duffle bag and said, "A'ight, fuck it. Let's slide on 'em."

**Chapter 29

Pacing a tight circle in the small, cluttered kitchen, gripping his 9mm Ruger in one hand and his smartphone in the other, Vic Walkson was thinking of what it would mean to his family and children if he was charged and convicted for the Marriott hotel murder.

Bria and her friend Kim were sitting at the kitchen table with TJ, a short dark-skinned nigga with dreadlocks who'd apparently just gotten bonded out of Marion County Jail, and a friend of his named Cornbread. They had their own guns on the table, though with the amount of rust and tape that covered the raggedy old pistols, V-Walk doubted they would work.

TJ was mad about his Suburban being crashed.

"...And then you left the fuckin' scene?!" TJ was saying. "That's a hit-and-run, you dumb ass bitch! You done fucked my shit up! Fresh out the county wit' four felonies hangin' over my head, and this the shit I gotta come home to? How in the fuck am I supposed to get some money in that hot ass truck? Stupid ass bitch, go pull it around back. Park it in the garage or somethin'. Ol' dumb ass."

"I'll pay for it," V-Walk said. "Whatever it cost, I'll pay for it all."

TJ looked at V-Walk. Then he looked at the gun in

V-Walk's hand.

"Who the fuck is this nigga anyway? You fuckin' niggas already?"

Bria shook her head and wiped the tears from her face. She and Kim were still crying over Kierra's death. "Stop it, TJ," she said. "His brother is the one who gave me the money to get your black ass out of jail this morning. You need to be thanking him, not talking shit."

Again TJ looked at Vic; V-Walk saw the look out of the corner of his eye as he dialed his brother's number again. He took a rubber-banded pile of hundreds out of his jacket pocket and dropped it on the table. "That's about twenty-five thousand. Do you."

TJ's anger disappeared very suddenly. His friend Cornbread's mood also seemed to brighten at the sight of so much money.

"Bruh," B-Walk answered, "you ain't gon believe what just happened. The nigga Baby Mike tried to up on me. Went in the glove compartment and grabbed a strap."

"What?! Man, what the fuck is goin' on today? This shit crazy."

"It's all good, bruh. We just gotta get the fuck outta Nap right now. Where you at in Haughville?"

"At the white house on the corner of 12th and Medford."

"I'm right down the street. Be there in like two

minutes, bruh."

Ending the call, V-Walk took a deep breath and forced himself to think clearly. He leaned back on the refrigerator, thinking.

Then the front door in the living room was hit so hard that the doorframe splintered.

A battering ram? A boot?

V-Walk wasn't sure, and before he could ponder too much about it gunshots rang out, riddling the door with holes.

Today was not a good day for Bria's friends.

Kim caught a bullet to the stomach and doubled over in her chair.

TJ and Cornbread picked up their pistols and sent a few shots at the front door as everyone took off running for the back door.

Cornbread was right behind V-Walk as TJ busted through the rear screen door ahead of him.

Just as V-Walk glanced back over his shoulder, a bullet exited through Cornbread's chin and sent the young light-complexioned man to the floor of the wooden back porch.

TJ and Bria ran in one direction, and V-Walk heard more thunderous gunshots as he ran down the alleyway in the opposite direction, praying to God that he would live to hug his children another day.

**Chapter 30

Rita's phone wouldn't stop lighting up on the bedside table.

Flako was calling.

FBI Agent Sneed was calling.

Alexus was calling.

Dr. Farr was calling.

But every call went unanswered, because Rita was in bed at her Trump penthouse with her Bible and a mug of coffee and she wasn't in the mood to talk to anyone but the Lord.

She was worried. Deeply worried.

She got a few chapters into Proverbs before succumbing to the overwhelming need to pray.

"Lord, I have a feeling that my trials and tribulations aren't over yet. I understand what I've gotten myself into by leading a corporation that gained its billions illegally. All I ask is that You look after my daughter when this life of mine ends. Keep her and my grandchildren out of harm's way. Shower them with blessings. In Jesus' name I pray, amen."

She heard King Neal and Savaria arguing just outside her bedroom door.

"Will you two please stop it," she said, sitting up.

A second later Vari burst into the room holding a broken pair of headphones in her hand and wearing the angriest pout a little girl has ever worn. King was right behind her, arms crossed and frowning.

"Grandma...I'm telling you now...if this little...ugh...if he breaks one more thing of mine, I'm going to find the tallest flight of stairs in the whole wide world and kick his little butt right down them."

"King, don't break your sister's —" Rita started.

But then King pulled a leg back and kicked Vari hard in the side of her right ankle.

"Ow!" Vari gave King a forceful shove, and he hit the back of his head on the corner of the door on the way down.

Vari dropped to the floor with him, holding her ankle as tears filled her eyes. King held the back of his head and cried.

It all happened in an instant.

"You kids are the worst." Rita swung her legs over the bedside and slipped her feet into her Gucci house shoes. She picked King up, rubbed the back of his head, and sat with him on the bed. "Get up, Vari. Sit right here." She patted the spot on the bed to the right of her, since King was on her left with his head on her shoulder.

"He kicked me," Vari sat on the bed, crossed her aching ankle over her knee, and continued to massage the spot where she'd been kicked.

There was a small knot growing on the back of King's head. Rita gave it a kiss and another gentle rub. She put her arms around their shoulders and pulled them closer.

"I'm going to tell you two a story that my mother once told my sister and I when we were fighting a lot."

She waited for the sobbing to fade away into sniffles. Her smartphone simply would not stop ringing, so she turned

"Once upon a time there was a little girl with a little brother she always fought. Every day they argued and scrapped like cats and dogs. Everything the little boy did angered his sister."

"Sounds about right," Vari said, and shot a baleful glance in King's direction.

He regarded her with the same cold look.

"Well," Rita continued, " one day their mommy and daddy went out to eat and never returned. Now the little girl and her brother had no parents, and they went to other people's homes to live, mean people who hated them both even more than the little girl hated her brother.

"Every day these people beat on the little girl and her brother. They fed the little girl and her brother food that not even a dog would want to eat. They made the little girl and her brother sleep on cold, dirty floors instead of warm, clean beds. They never bought the little girl and her brother any gifts for birthdays and holidays. I mean, these people were terrible, you get what I'm saying?"

Vari nodded her head yes. Her expression was serious now. So was King's.

"On all those sleepless nights without their parents, the little girl would lie awake on the cold floor with her little brother, the brother she'd once hated so darned much. Now he was the only family she had in a world full of mean grownups..."

"And?" asked Vari.

"You tell me the rest of the story," Rita said to Savaria. "What would you do if that little girl was you? Would you still hate your brother if nobody else in the whole world loved you? One day that question will need an answer, Vari. One day it'll be just you and your brother in a world full of mean grownups. If you want someone who really loves you to have your back when nobody else does, you two had better start loving each other before it's too late."

King stared across Rita's lap at his big sister. "I sorry, Vari. I won't kick you again, I promise."

"Sure you won't," Vari said with a sarcastic smirk. "I'm sorry too, brother."

"If that ever happens to us would you still be mean to me?" There was no smirk now. King meant business.

"No, King. You're my brother. I love you sooooo much. You just get on my nerves sometimes, that's all."

"Nerves?" Rita laughed once and shook her head. "Will you two devils go somewhere and let me be now? Go out there and tell Britney to turn on a movie for us to watch. I'll be out in a few minutes."

"Can we watch the one about the man with the hammer?" King asked.

"No," Vari said as the two of them ran out of the room, "we gon' watch the black Cinderella."

"That's for girls!" was the last thing Rita heard King shout before she closed her door and went to her bedside table to tend to her smartphone.

She returned Alexus's call first, not only because her daughter was most important, but also because Alexus was sure to know what everyone else was calling about.

**Chapter 31

Alexus was far too distraught to speak to anyone other than her mother, so seeing Rita's chocolate brown face pop up on her iPhone was a blessing.

She was back in her hotel suite, studying her tear-streaked face in the mirror over the sink in the fairly spacious bathroom. Mercedes was on the toilet; the sound of her peeing was so embarrassingly loud that Alexus waited for the flow of urine to slow before answering the phone.

"What in the world is going on, Alexus?" Rita wasted no time in getting to the point. "Your uncle Flako has been calling me like crazy. I caught that FBI agent following me earlier, and now he's calling, too. Tell me something."

Alexus noticed her hands were shaking. A seemingly endless supply of tears were sliding down her face, destroying her makeup and the new white Chanel dress she'd selected for the day.

"It's about that guy who has the same name as Papi," she said, sniffling. "The terrorist guy. They believe he may be in Chicago. Sneed and his men have been following you since early this morning when they first heard of it. It's what Flako was trying to tell you."

"Why couldn't you just tell me? And are you crying? Jesus Christ, you're worse than these kids.

What is it? You and Blake at odds again?"

"I'm fine, Momma. Just be safe. Keep the kids in the house until we can get some more info on this guy. No unnecessary trips."

"I'm really getting fed up with all this mess, Alexus. You need to leave that lifestyle alone. Aren't you rich enough? Seriously, how much more money can you possibly make?"

"It isn't about the money anymore, Ma. It's all about the power. I'm what every drug-dealer has ever wanted to be. I'm like Pablo Escobar to the tenth power. Hell, I'm the cocaine queen. I'm the best who's ever done it."

Rita laughed. "Your arrogance reminds me so much of your father."

"I know."

"Don't end up like him."

"I won't."

"You sure about that?"

"Absolutely." Alexus turned her back to the sink and stepped aside so Mercedes could wash her hands.

"If you ever go down," Rita said, "I'm not going down with you. I hope you know that. I'm not built for prison."

"I'd never pull you down with me. You'll need to be around to take care of King and Vari if something ever happens to me and that black bastard I was stupid enough to marry."

Drying her hands, Mercedes said, "She pulled a gun on Blake to stop him and his friend from shooting me. He got mad about it and left."

"Snitch," Alexus hissed at her sister.

Rita gasped. "Is that what happened? Why'd he pull a gun on her?"

"It's a long story."

"You all have issues."

"Tell me something I don't know."

Mercedes took a tissue out of her Michael Kors bag and dabbed at Alexus's tears. For a moment no one spoke. Alexus thought of Blake and wondered if he'd ever forgive her for taking her sister's side.

She prayed that he would.

"Be safe," Rita said finally. "I'm about to watch some movies with the kids. Oh, before I forget, King's got a big knot on the back of his head. He kicked Vari and she pushed him into the door. They're fine now, though."

"OMG."

"I'll call you in a few. Tell Flako and Sneed it's my off day. I'm not taking any calls, no matter how many terrorists they believe are in Chicago."

Alexus snickered as the call ended. She fixed her face with a bit of makeup, while Mercedes used the same kit to conceal the facial bruises she'd gotten on the jet.

"We don't need those niggas. Fuck a man," Mercedes said. "We'll do fine by ourselves."

Alexus didn't agree, so she didn't reply.

**Chapter 32

The shiny white Bugatti Galibier rocketed down the highway leaving Indianapolis.

An hour later it veered onto the Exit 34B off-ramp that led into Blake's hometown of Michigan City, Indiana.

Biggs was driving.

Blake was sipping Lean, rolling Kush, and rocking back and forth to the Chief Keef song that was booming from the car's speakers.

'...I'm a gorilla in a fuckin' coupe

Finna pull up to da zoo, nigga

Ooh, nigga, who da fuck is you?

I don't new, nigga

No, nigga, pull up on yo block, we gon blow, nigga

Go nigga, run nigga, run for da po nigga!

Gas what I smoke, nigga

Feds at my door jump out da window, nigga

No you can't get no money you silly hoe

I just hit a stang, Faneto...'

"Man, I love this song," Blake said, taking in a lungful of smoke.

"How in the fuck can you like any of that nigga's songs after all the gunplay y'all went through?"

"I love that gang shit. If we catch some of them opp ass niggas out here in MC we bussin' just like we did in Nap. I know I am."

Biggs pulled into a BP gas station to fill up the tank just as a burnt orange Hummer on large rims of the same color was leaving the pump.

The car at the pump in front of them was a maroon Nissan. A middle aged white man was pumping the gas; three small children were playing around in the backseat.

There were two other vehicles parked at the pumps: a red Chevy van and a white Navigator that looked like it needed a wash more than it needed gas. A big-bootied black woman in gray sweatpants was wobbling her way out of the driver's seat of the van, while a sexy-figured younger girl (judging from her looks, Blake guessed she was the thicker woman's daughter) hopped out of the passenger door with her eyes on the Bugatti.

When Blake pushed open his door and stepped out she screamed.

"Bulletface! Ma, look! It's Bulletface!"

Blake grinned and gave them a wave. The mother-daughter duo came over for a selfie. He reached in the car and grabbed a copy of his last album to sign for the girl, who introduced herself as Dominique.

"I'm eighteen, by the way," she said.

Her mother, Donna, raised a hand and said, "Thirty-one. And yeah, I had her young. I was thirteen. I went to school with your brother Streets. Shit, man, what are you doing out here? And without security?" Then she glanced at the big Desert Eagle in his shoulder holster and said, "Oh."

A couple of years prior, after being acquitted on a bevy of murder charges, Blake had managed to secure an Indiana gun license.

It was all the security he needed.

Dominique trailed him into the gas station while her mother pumped gas. A Hispanic girl who looked to be about Dominique's age was behind the counter, and three black girls were in back at the refrigerators, chatting and trying to decide which sodas they would purchase. They seemed grown, though not much older than Dominique, and one of them — her face looked familiar, but Blake couldn't remember her name — had more ass than Donna.

Everyone stopped what they were doing when they saw Blake and focused solely on him. He heard murmurs of "Girl, that's Bulletface!" and "That is Bulletface!" and "Go over there and talk to him!" as he picked up two packs of Skittles and walked to the refrigerators for a few cold Sprites to mix with his Promethazine and Codeine.

Biggs was at his side a moment later, eyeing the

girls with his ever-present smile. They knew he'd recently signed to Blake's record label, and they were just as excited to see him.

As expected, the three girls (Blake would later learn that their names were Tameka, Shakeyla, and Candice) approached Blake, and he had no problem taking pictures with them before making his way to the counter to add a 36-count value pack of Magnums to his order.

"Where y'all 'bout to go?" one of them asked.

Biggs answered without hesitation: "Wherever y'all goin'."

"We' all goin' to Donna's party in Southgate."

"Well," Biggs said, "Donna's party it is."

And that is how their evening began.

****Chapter 33

"Why are we here, Alberto? Are you that serious about wanting to meet this woman?"

"I am," Juan said.

After calling just about every luxury hotel in Indianapolis and studying their Google images, Juan Costilla had checked Alexus's Instagram page again, and sure enough there was a photo of her in the hotel lobby at the Indianapolis Marriott East. The photo had been uploaded just thirty-four minutes prior.

Juan had driven up to the valet in a small BMW he purchased on Craigslist for $5,300. It was clean, as was his suit and tie and the knockoff Gucci dress he'd bought in Chicago for Maryann.

Now, sitting next to Maryann in the lobby with a DuPont Registry magazine open in his hands, Juan Costilla was impatiently waiting for Alexus to exit the hotel. He found it ironic that Alexus was being stalked by a man with the same name as the man who'd fathered her.

"So," Maryann asked, scratching at her inner forearm, "what am I to do now? Get an autograph? From Alexus?"

He nodded. "Yes. I'll give you an ink pen, you go and get her to sign her name with the ink pen, and when you hand me that signature I'll give you five grand and take you back to Chicago. Simple as that."

"Sounds simple enough," Maryann reasoned.

"It's very simple. A child could do it."

"I'm not exactly the smartest blonde, you know."

"I know."

"Hey!" she slapped his arm and laughed jubilantly. "You're not supposed to agree with me, you a-hole." She extended a palm. "Give me the ink pen."

"Not yet."

"Why not?"

"Because you're not exactly the smartest blonde. Said so yourself."

"I'll remember that the next time you want your dick sucked."

Juan ignored the snide remark and continued to peruse the luxury homes in the magazine. He took no real interest in the multimillion dollar homes, but studying them seemed like the best possible cover at the moment.

"This might just be the easiest five thousand dollars I've ever made," Maryann said, again clawing at her forearm. "You wouldn't happen to have seventy-five cents, would you? Or a dollar?" She pointed at the Pepsi vending machine across the marble-floored lobby.

"Don't you have any discipline? Sit still. She'll be down here any minute."

"I'm thirsty, Alberto. Jeez."

Juan gritted his teeth. He couldn't wait for this to be over. He had a nasty little surprise for this trifling slut. It was the only reason he hadn't cut off her head when she'd sauntered up to his rental car seeking a quick trick.

He dug in his slacks and retrieved a couple of singles.

Maryann dashed off as soon as she got the dollars in her hand.

**Chapter 34

God had sent Vic Walkson an angel in Indianapolis, an angel in the form of his very own brother. Brian had screeched to a stop at the end of the alleyway just as V-Walk made it there. Instead of running around the monster truck and hopping in the passenger seat, V-Walk had leapt into the backseat on the driver's side and stayed there until they were well out of Haughville.

On the highway they had discussed their troublesome day at length and come to the conclusion that Blake had to have been behind it all.

Brian drove to Michigan City, stopped at the BP gas station (where they met and exchanged numbers with three girls who were on their way to some lady named Donna's party), and then went to their mother's old house on Holiday Street.

No one lived in the one-story clapboard home, though it was fully furnished, with utilities paid up for the next two years and a Broadview security system that included outdoor and indoor cameras.

In the basement is where the Walkson brothers had stashed the stolen shipment of cocaine bricks.

Brian and Vic sat on the leather couch in the living room and rolled up two fat blunts for the long talk they were about to have. They kept all the lights off; only the dim glow of the setting sun illuminated the room.

"I know it's kinda late to be changing my mind," Brian began, " but maybe we should be after Blake's wife instead of chasing him down. He was in a coma when bruh got killed. Ain't no way he could've sent somebody at bruh when he was in a coma."

"Yeah, but I bet he's the one who sent Baby Mike at you. I bet he's the reason that nigga tried to off me at the hotel. Shit, it might've even been him who shot up Bria's house. We gotta get"— Vic coughed half a dozen times and passed the blunt to Brian — "get that nigga out the way, folks. I don't think we can get Alexus but we can try to do that too."

"We can get that bitch. The same way we got her dope. It won't take too much to get Mercedes to set the shit up. She said she hate her sister anyway. You know she done lost her whole family fuckin' around with them rich people. She hate all of em. Why you think she was so willing to set up that robbery in California for us? Getting her to set up Alexus will be just as easy."

"She was supposed to set Blake up in Nap, though," Vic pointed out. "Look how that turned out. I damn near got killed —twice! You almost got killed. Fuck that bitch, she can get it too."

"I know, bruh," said Brian.

A moment of silence ensued. Brian was thinking. Vic was thinking. They had enough wealth to live happily for the remainder of their days, but neither of them could go on living life without first avenging their youngest brother's murder.

"Let's focus on selling those bricks first," V-Walk said finally. "No more rushing to get at that nigga. We'll take our time, think out every detail. Mercedes said he caught Shawnna and Donny before they could get to him in New York. If they talked, he probably knows who sent them. Let's just lay low and get money for a few weeks. See how shit goes. Then we'll get Mercedes to make another play, and this time we won't fuck it up."

Brian nodded his head in agreement and lifted his smartphone. "That's what we'll do. Fuck it." He dialed a number.

"Who you calling?" Vic asked.

"Them hoes from the gas station." Brian put the phone to his ear. "They said somethin' about a party."

**Chapter 35

'Ass fat, yea I know
You just got cash, blow some mo'
Blow some mo', blow some mo'
The more you spend it, the faster it go
Bad bitches, on the floor, its rainin' hunnids
Throw some mo', throw some mo'
Throw some mo', throw some mo'

Hi, bye hater, I flood the club with paper
Shorty got an ass some for now and some for later,
(delicious)

Something like Nicki's, dancin' like Maliah

How I'm throwing all this money, I'ma fuck around
and buy her

I can flick the money all night til' my wrist tired
(tired)
If you put in work, this the night you gon' retire
(retire)
You a bad bitch, I ain't even gon' deny ya
She told me throw that money, I said make it worth
my while
I'm bout to empty out the ATM, (throw it throw it
throw it)

She doin' tricks that make a nigga wanna spend,
(blow it, blow it)
Girl you know you got me fascinated,
Just keep on dancin' til I'm outta paper, (never)...'

One phone call was all it took for Blake to bring out the whole city and the biggest ballers from the surrounding cities, including the Vice Lords and Gangster Disciples he used to serve kilos to in Gary, South Bend, Ft. Wayne, and Chicago; video models strippers he'd made it rain on at one time or another; hood girls and college girls. Nobody was too busy for Bulletface.

The music came courtesy of the six 12-inch speakers in the trunk of his close friend Fly's 1972 Chevy Caprice "Donk", which was just one in a long line of old- and new-schools on big chrome rims that took up all the parking spaces in front of Donna's apartment building.

Biggs had his sights set on Tameka, one of the girls from the gas station, as she twerked and bounced her ass to the Rae Sremmurd song with about thirty other intoxicated girls.

Blake's eyes were on Dominique. She too was twerking, only instead of dancing on the sidewalk with the other girls she was dancing against him on the porch. Standing with them were Biggs, Donna, and Nona, Biggs's younger sister and Blake's ex.

Needless to say, Nona wasn't too happy to see another woman's ass jiggling against the crotch of her ex's $5,000 Balmain jeans.

The four white diamond necklaces dangling from Blake's neck and the white and black diamond MBM pendants attached to them were each worth twenty times the price of the jeans. The chunky white diamonds on his pinkies were worth $140,000 each. He'd sent a few of the girls to the liquor store with $5,000 and ordered them to get 100 bottles of Ciroc and keep the change. Another $3,500 had gone to BD-Raw, a gold-mouthed dope boy Blake had done business with a few times in the past, for a pound of Kush that now had the entire apartment complex reeking of loud smoke. A few more racks had gone to feeding the crowd— everything from McDonald's and Burger King to Pizza Hut and some locally owned restaurants.

After eating a bunch of hot wings and pizza, Blake had shunned the liquor and stuck to his Lean, as did Biggs and a few other guys.

The disdain in Nona's eyes was evident as she watched Dominique treat her ex-lover like a stripper pole.

Blake's dick was rock-hard, and Dominique's ass felt big and soft against it.

Nona grew angrier by the minute.

"Girl," she said, "I don't know why you dancin' all up on him like that. The nigga ain't gon' do shit but fuck you and leave you. He might — and that's a strong might— give you a couple dollars, but that's about it." She sucked her teeth and rolled her eyes.

Standing there with the backs of her meaty thighs on the porch railing, in an expensive-looking gray mini-dress and tall black Louboutin heels, Nona looked the epitome of elegance and good taste, while at the same time possessing the protuberant curves of a hip hop magazine model. She was angry, but she was still unbearably attractive.

Blake grinned at Nona, biting his lower lip.

Dominique paid the derogatory comments no mind; she stuck to displaying her sexiest smile and popping her ass on the front of his pants. She knew that, in her skintight shirt and jeans and Air Max sneakers, she was just as bad as Nona— not nearly as thick, but certainly as eye-catching in beauty.

Glancing around the vast parking lot, Blake saw a number of smartphones aimed in his direction.

The first thing that came to mind was TMZ.

Then Media Takeout.

He'd been on both of them too many times to count because of situations like this, and knowing Alexus, if she saw it on TMZ tonight she'd have Dominique dead by morning.

Picking up his duffle from the concrete stair behind him, Blake curled an arm around Dominique's waist, pulled her back into the apartment, and walked backward through the tan-carpeted living room and into the

cramped bathroom.

She never got to turn to face him.

He pushed the door shut and moved forward against her, tossing back another swallow of Lean, dropping the duffle bag, and rubbing between her thighs with his free hand, pressing the concealed tip of his erection against her pillowy cheeks.

He set down the Styrofoams and his burning blunt on the sink and planted a trail of tender kisses down the nape of her neck.

She put the side of her face on the wooden door and stared at his reflection in the oval-shaped mirror over the sink.

"Boy, stop rubbing me right there...or pull out that dick and give it to me."

Grin widening, Blake reached in the duffle and ripped into his box of condoms. He hurriedly opened one and slid it on as Dominique undid her Hermes belt and pushed her pants and red lace panties down to her knees.

He put his hands on her waist and slowly prodded the head of his twelve-inch love muscle in and out of her.

Her face tightened.

"Ooo, shit," she said with quiet intensity.

He went in deeper, again biting his lip. But this time he wasn't grinning. It was a carnal bite of the lip, accompanied by a strong thrust that buried the majority of his length inside her.

She squealed and whimpered as he began to fuck her, pressing the palms of her hands on the door and looking back at him. Her pussy was so tight that it felt almost as if he was copulating with a keyhole.

The Lean had him in such a daze that he hardly realized so much time — twenty-seven minutes to be exact — had passed before he gushed a wad of semen into the Magnum.

By then Dominique's legs were just as rubbery as the used condom.

She pulled up her jeans and slumped down to the floor, breathing hard and gawking at Blake with her mouth and eyes wide open.

He flushed the condom and sat on the toilet, gripping and stroking his deflating phallus in his hand.

"Come on," he said. "Round two."

"Shiiiiit." Dominique laughed.

"I'm serious," Blake persisted.

"Boy, you are not about to kill me up in here. I know you're known for killing people, but I won't be added to that list."

"Come on, lil mama. I ain't gon' hurt you. Suck on this muhfucka or somethin'." He held his long sex weapon at its base and shook a globule of cum off the tip of it. "And I'm not known for killing nobody. Don't believe everything you hear."

"Oh, please. I know all about you, Bulletface. Everybody does. Kollege Kidd talks about you like DJ Akademiks talks about Chiraq savages. You're a gun-crazy young savage." She stood up, buckling her belt. "But don't worry." She walked to him. "I'm not scared. Believe it or not"— she kneeled down between his parted legs and wrapped her fingers around his dick as if it were a broomstick— "it actually turns me on. I like that gangsta shit."

She stared up at him. Her tongue flickered on the underside of his dick. He balled her ponytail in his fist and tried to force himself into her throat, but she knocked his hand away started sucking him at her own pace.

He reached over and grabbed his Styrofoams and the blunt. Relighting the Kush, he grinned affectionately at the caramel-skinned girl's pretty face as she sucked him, simultaneously slathering his length with saliva and jerking him in her hands.

When his iPhone rang a minute later, he had the overwhelming inclination to pay it no mind.

But a brief glance at it showed him that it was Biggs calling, so he answered.

"Bruh! The nigga V-Walk just pulled up!" Biggs said in complete disbelief.

Fuck my life, Blake thought, pulling the Desert Eagle from its holster.

**Chapter 36

Alexus was the queen of all queens in a full-length white mink coat and five-inch Chanel heels that were covered in white diamonds. Right beside her, Mercedes donned a black mink and Giuseppe Zanotti heels that were blinged out in black diamonds. They were like twins wearing opposite colors.

Surrounded by bodyguards on the elevator, they were about to leave the hotel and go to a Kevin Hart show at the Bankers Life Fieldhouse stadium, then they would go out to eat and enjoy themselves a night out on the town, since their significant others had jumped ship earlier in the day.

Observing herself in the solid reflection of the elevator doors, Alexus put on a huge fake smile.

On the inside she felt empty. It was like Blake had somehow managed to take her heart with him when he left.

"Don't look so sad, sis," Mercedes said, giving Alexus a quick one-armed hug. "We'll make it through this shit. I'm from Chicago, and you're from Texas. Can't nobody break us or make us. Fuck Biggs, and fuck Blake, too. They'll be crawling back to us in no time. I ain't never had a nigga leave me. We're some bad bitches. And we got money. If they don't come back it's their loss, you feel me? No need in stressing over it when we can get whatever man we want."

"Fuck love," Alexus murmured. "If this shit with Blake doesn't work out I might just go gay like Tee Tee did."

"Speaking of Tee Tee," Mercedes said, "I'm trying to figure out why these girls I know keep asking about what happened to her and Tasia."

Eyebrows knitted, Alexus looked at Mercedes with questioning eyes. "What girls? What's their names?"

"Fanny is one of them. The other's a stripper in Atlanta. Think her stripper name's Baddie Barbie. I've been serving them for a while now."

Alexus squinted as she thought back to earlier in the day when she'd caught Blake scrolling down some girl's Instagram page. She'd glimpsed the name before quickly turning to look the other way.

It was definitely Baddie Barbie, or something close to it.

As the elevator dinged and the doors parted, Alexus went to Instagram on her iPhone to search for the stripper.

"Blake's thirsty ass was just liking that hoe's pics and shit," she said. "For all we know the bitch could be trying to set him up. She might be some kin to Tee Tee or Tasia."

Shaking her head as she followed Enrique out of the elevator and into the hotel lobby, Alexus made up her mind to call Blake about the stripper. If he didn't answer she'd leave a voicemail. She knew that this was an argument she'd win hands down. Next time his dumb ass would think twice before thirsting for an Instagram thot.

She made it to the girl's page and gasped in shock.

The girl looked exactly like her old friend Tasia Olsen, whom Blake had shot to death in Matamoros, Mexico.

"How didn't he notice this?" Alexus muttered vacantly. She took a screenshot of the page and was just about to send it to Blake's phone along with an old picture of Tasia when a white girl in a fake Gucci dress began shouting her name from across the lobby.

"Alexus Costilla! Alexus! Can I please get an autograph?" The girl was moving fast, wagging an ink pen between two fingers.

Enrique held up a hand to stop the young woman, but Alexus pushed his arm down.

"It's fine, Enrique. I'll sign—"

Alexus didn't get to finish her sentence.

The ink pen that the girl was wagging between two fingers was a bomb.

The explosion was catastrophic.

**Chapter 37

Blake stepped into the doorway with his gun in hand and stood next to Biggs.

If not for the police car that had just appeared in the court where Donna's party was going down, Blake would have opened fire on the chameleon-painted Hummer as soon as he saw it.

But he didn't, of course. He wasn't trying to spend the rest of his life in prison, and there seemed to be no immediate threat.

V-Walk and a dark-skinned man who Blake guessed was the other Walkson brother were talking to a few of the girls while staring directly at Blake and Biggs.

Blake holstered his big golden gun and stared at the two men.

"Well," Biggs said with a laugh, "guess the nigga lived through that shit in Nap."

"I should start blowin' right muhfuckin now." Blake gritted his teeth cantankerously. Most of his guys were too drunk and high to notice the Walkson brothers.

However, a few of his close friends — namely D-Rock, .45, and AJ from his Dub Life crew; and Batman, Rube, and Killa, some Vice Lords from Gary he'd grown close to over the years.— peeped the situation for what it was and moved closer to Blake.

All he had to do was give them the word.

"Ay, Vic!" he shouted. "Let me get a word with you right quick!"

"Nah, ain't no words, nigga!" was all Victor Walkson got out before the gunshots began.

Batman and Rube— two dark-hued Mafia Insane Vice Lords with long dreadlocks and necks full of gold chains— pulled handguns with 30-round clips from their hips and started blasting, sending all the girls screaming and running for cover.

This time the Walkson brothers weren't lacking.

As Blake was drawing his Desert Eagle (and wishing he hadn't left his Mac-11 in his duffle bag in the bathroom), he witnessed a masked man run out from behind the building Batman and Rube were standing in front of with an assault rifle aimed at the back of Batman's head.

At the same time, the Walkson brothers reached into the Hummer and snatched out two AK-47s.

V-Walk started shooting at Blake and Biggs just as the masked gunman blew Batman's brains free from his skull. Blake shot back as he and Biggs ducked into the apartment with Donna and Nona.

Kicking the door shut, Blake's eyes went wide as he watched the door get riddled with bullets.

He heard Dominique and Nona screaming their

lungs out behind him. The tall window next to the door shattered and rained glass down on him. Biggs's Mac-11 was booming a few feet to the right of him, carving a line of holes in the living room wall and blowing out the large picture window.

He turned around, crouching low, and took off running to the bathroom to get his own Mac. Nona and Dominique made it there first, but they made a right and disappeared down a flight of stairs to the basement.

"Bruh!" Blake shouted. "Get the fuck in here, nigga! Get from in front of that window!"

Outside the gunfire continued, a thunderous applause of blazing machine guns and handguns mixed with police sirens and screeching tires to create a cacophony of chaos that had Blake's adrenaline rushing through his every vein.

Rushing back to the door with his own submachine gun, he had to step over Biggs, who'd suffered a bullet wound to his left forearm and another to his left thigh. The gunshots quieted into nothing but the shrieking tires of escaping vehicles and the agonizing screams of the wounded. The jingle of his smartphone ringing broke through the noise, but he ignored it and swung the door open to get back to the gunfight.

He caught sight of the Hummer as it whipped around the corner onto Southwind Drive and sped off down the road. Twenty-two men and twelve women were lying on the pavement in growing pools of blood, and the others were either running off on foot or speeding out of the apartment complex in their cars.

There were two police cars now; four white men in blue uniforms were advancing toward Donna's apartment with their guns trained on Blake.

"Put the guns down! Now!" the officers barked in unison.

In that fleeting moment Blake thought of Mike Brown, the eighteen-year-old who was killed last year in Ferguson, Missouri.

Instinctively, he dropped the gun and put his hands up.

"Don't shoot!" he said.

In military formation, the policemen moved forward and took Blake into custody.

**Chapter 38

The next morning was worse than the night prior for Blake.

He woke up in a holding cell full of hungover men — four white guys and a black teen with a face full of tattoos and a mouthful of gold teeth— who had all enjoyed themselves a little too much last night.

He didn't talk to any of them.

After breakfast trays were served, he and the gold-mouthed teen were moved to North-8, a cell block that housed Laporte County Jail's violent offenders.

He'd done numerous stints in the jail before. Usually everyone but the old heads were asleep until around noon when lunch was served.

This morning was different.

The circular clock on the wall near the shower stalls read 7:21 when Blake entered the block with his Rubbermaid tote box and mattress. The officer said, "Both of you, cell one." and shut the heavy green door behind them.

The cell block had only four cells, four men to each room; there were 14 black men standing and sitting at the four octagonal steel tables in the dayroom. Their eyes left the television (a quick glance told Blake that they were watching CNN) and settled on Blake.

He knew most of them. Old school Remo, who'd been in the same cell block with Blake twice in the past, was here. Rico G, a GD from Blake's old neighborhood, was sitting at a table playing spades with Remo and two younger drug-dealers from the hood.

No one spoke.

They simply shifted their attention back to the TV, which was mounted high on the wall.

Blake dropped the plastic box and mattress beside a table and watched the television with them.

"Over the last half hour we have received a number of conflicting reports, but a source close to the family has confirmed to us here at CNN that Alexus and Mercedes Costilla were both critically injured as a result of the injuries they suffered in a suicide bombing at a Marriott hotel in Indianapolis yesterday evening.

"On another sour note, Alexus Costilla's husband, Blake King, known to the rap world as Bulletface, has been arrested and charged with one count of murder and two counts of attempted murder in his hometown of Michigan City, Indiana following a shooting that has reportedly left four dead and thirty others wounded. According to police reports, a heated argument between Bulletface and two other men led to the deadly shootout. The police report alleges that Bulletface aimed a gun at officers before finally surrendering.

"But the problems for Alexus don't stop there. A five-year DEA and ATF joint investigation that spanned from Mexico over into Texas and California — and allegedly spreading all across the country from those two states— has ended with the arrests of over five hundred men and women. One of the men arrested is Pedro Costilla, Alexus Costilla's cousin. Federal authorities are alleging that Pedro is an underboss of a Mexican drug cartel that is currently in control of every drug cartel in Mexico. The Costilla Cartel— known previously as the Matamoros Cartel— reportedly struck a deal with other cartels late last year that gave them complete power over all cocaine smuggling into the United States."

There was a dramatic pause as Anderson Cooper straightened his slender black tie and stared fixedly into the camera.

"At the head of it all is Costilla Corp. CEO Alexus Costilla,' he continued, "the woman America knows as a corporate mogul, now suspected of being the top boss of the Costilla Cartel. The lengthy investigation reveals how Alexus and the Costilla Cartel have been able to move tons of cocaine and marijuana and billions of dollars in drug money in and out of the country via a drug tunnel and ten submarines that dozens of crooked DEA and FBI agents allegedly knew of for years. It is also alleged that those crooked agents took payments and helped insure that the drug shipments would go undiscovered as thousands of kilos were shipped all across the country.

"Alexus Costilla has been flown to UCLA Medical Center in Los Angeles to undergo an emergency surgery for the injuries sustained in the suicide bombing, but she is already under arrest and facing a staggering four hundred and eighty-six federal indictments. She will be handcuffed to the hospital bed and under watch by US Secret Service members until she's deemed fit for jail..."

"I ain't pointed no fuckin' gun at nobody," Blake muttered, gritting his white diamond teeth.

That little lie was actually the least of Blake's worries, but he didn't want to admit to himself just how torn he was emotionally about Alexus's condition and the indictments she was now facing. Better to dwell on the small problems when the big ones were too heavy to bear.

Even so, his eyes grew watery as the image of Alexus lying in a hospital bed swept across his mind's theater.

He knew that the other inmates had a million and one questions for him; instead of speaking with them, he went to the payphone and dialed Attorney Britney Bostic's cell phone number. He knew it by heart. She'd been his and Alexus's lawyer for years now.

As soon as she accepted the collect call, he said, "Am I named in any of those indictments?"

"No. But you don't have a bond. I'm on my way to the courthouse to pick up the arrest report myself, then I'll be down to see you."

"Where are my kids?"

"They'll be fine. Rita's taken them to the Versace Mansion. They're saying that the ISIS executioner suspected of beheading those journalists and aid workers in Syria may have been behind the bombing. A man seen leaving the hotel in a BMW is wanted for questioning. He gave the girl the ink pen that exploded."

"And Mercedes is fucked up too, huh?"

"Yeah. Really it was the bodyguards who got it worst. Mercedes was in between Alexus and the girl with the explosive, got the short end of the stick. She has burns all over her body. Alexus has some burns on her legs, shrapnel lacerations, and a few broken bones. Enrique's got severe burns and he lost a hand. It's like all this was planned to go down just as they unveiled the federal indictments and started raiding all our offices. Pedro's in custody. All of Costilla Corp's accounts have been frozen."

"What about my accounts?"

"You're fine so far. And they can't touch Alexus's money because legally half of it belongs to you. I have some ideas as to why all this happened. We'll go over it when I get there. Should be in the next thirty minutes or so. Try to stay out of trouble. You have court at noon. I should be able to get you a bond."

"Just hurry up and get here," he said and hung up.

He dialed Rita's number, got no answer, and then he called his brother to let him know the situation.

Terrence "Streets" King had already learned of Blake's arrest.

"Was waiting on you to call me," he said. "Damn, bruh. You can't stay out that street shit for nothin'. Nigga, you're a billionaire! The fuck wrong with you? Learn to sit the fuck down sometimes."

"Bruh, I'm not tryna hear that shit," Blake said, again grinding his teeth together. "Get in contact with Rita to check on my kids. Tell Meach, Scrill, and Mocha I'm good and I'll call em later. I'm about to lay down for a li'l bit. Man, I can't believe this shit."

"Be safe. You know T-Walk's brothers got locked up last night, too."

Instinctively, Blake turned his back to the wall and studied the faces he'd hardly given a glance a few minutes earlier. He knew how the Walkson brothers looked; neither of them were present.

"What they get jammed up for?" he asked.

"For shooting all those people. Just read it. They got caught leavin'. Cops lookin' for the choppas they say got used in the shooting."

Blake nodded, still looking around the dayroom. "Catch you later, bruh. Check on my kids," he repeated before hanging up.

He took his property box and matt to cell one, where a bottom bunk was waiting. Remo said something to the others about giving him some alone time. He put his sheet and blanket on the mattress and lay there with his arms crossed, staring up at the steel underside of the top bunk and praying his wife would survive her injuries.

"Why in the fuck did I leave her there anyway," he muttered aloud to himself.

A part of him was stuck wanting to know why the U.S. government had suddenly turned on Alexus and the Costilla Cartel. He knew of numerous times the government had aided Alexus in laundering billions of dollars in drug money. NASA had even participated in the laundering in return for hundreds of millions in donations to their space program.

The investigation had to have gone deeper than Alexus could have ever imagined.

Blake hoped he'd get bonded out before his name joined the list of federal indictments.

He was waiting on his lawyer's visit when the tattoo-faced teen with the gold teeth walked in and threw his matt to the top bunk.

Just then, Blake heard a familiar female voice coming from the vent next to the toilet.

"Hey, anybody know what cell block B-Walk is in?"

**Chapter 39

The Walkson brothers were placed in cell one in North-4 block, two floors beneath North-8. Between the two male cell blocks was North-6, a female cell block.

Through the ventilation system next to the toilets in the first and second cells, inmates were able to communicate with those above and below them.

Brian was pissing when the girl shouted.

"Hey, anybody know what cell block B-Walk is in?"

Brian Walkson's eyes shot to the vent beside the stainless steel toilet.

"Helloooooo," the girl said. "I know you niggas woke. Somebody get on this damn vent and talk to me. And I'm a bad bitch so please no broke boys or nasty old men."

The voice belonged to Tameka, the girl B-Walk had called from his mother's old house after the conversation with Vic.

It had been Tameka who told him that Blake and Biggs were at the party in Southgate, giving them ample time to get a plan together.

A plan that had failed miserably.

Brian lay on his stomach and put his face by the

vent.

"Yo," he said, and laughed.

"What's funny?" Tameka asked.

"You. Bet you don't even know who this is."

"Umm, duhh. I'd have to be a psychic to know that."

"It's B-Walk."

A brief silence followed.

"B-Walk? For real?" She spoke in an incredulous whisper. "This Tameka. Damn, it's you? You good?"

"Yeah." Brian shifted around uncomfortably. "What they get you for?"

"I had a warrant for a dealing charge I caught a few weeks ago. Guess I sold to an undercover, fucking around on the dime. Police caught me running last night. Shit, I know Bulletface is sick. Did you see that dude with the mask on come out with a choppa and blast his guy in the head when they started shootin' at y'all?"

"Nah," he lied. The masked gunman had actually been his cousin Goldie. He'd given the AK-47 to Goldie and told him to stay out of sight until things got ugly.

"That shit was crazy," Tameka said.

"Yeah, it was."

"But fuck Bulletface if he had something to do

with T-Walk getting killed. T-Walk was my boo."

"Yeah, I miss bruh."

Sitting at the steel desk across the room, Vic began signaling for Brian to end the conversation. "Talk about something else," he mouthed. "Let's get in court first, nigga. Fuck around and have that bitch on the stand testifying against us."

Brian waved his brother off.

"I heard y'all millionaires," Tameka said. "You should look out and get me out of here. Especially since I told y'all where to find that nigga. My bond's only two thousand dollars."

"I'll see what I can do. But listen, lil mama, you can't be tellin' people I talked to you on the phone before that shit happened. Don't even let them hoes know we knew each other out there. Watch what you say on this vent. You know it's a nigga upstairs probably listening to us right now."

"Yeah, you right, you right." She sucked her teeth. "Y'all okay? Where yo brother at?"

"Hold on, I gotta get on the phone for a second. Be right back," B-Walk said.

He was lying again. He got up and sat at the other desk in the rear of the room. Resting his back on the wall, he stretched out a foot and shook his head.

"Stupid ass nigga," Vic said. "Don't get us ran up. We might be able to come from under this shit."

"I ain't gon get us jammed up, ni—"

"Well, shut the fuck up and stop talkin' to dat hoe."

Brian shook his head and clasped his hands together, a gesture of frustration.

Leaving the shooting scene last night, he had stopped around the corner from the apartment complex to pick up Goldie and ditch the assault rifles in a trashcan.

He'd stomped on the gas and screeched away immediately afterwards, but by the time he made it to an intersection on Ohio Street four blocks down, police cars were coming at him from every direction.

They all had jumped out and ran, him, Vic, and Goldie, but they hadn't gotten far.

The police had yet to find the guns; he and Vic were hoping it would stay that way.

As of now, they were charged with two counts of murder and fifteen counts of attempted murder.

Nikkia Staples, their attorney, was on her way to see them.

The Walkson brothers were praying for the best.

**Chapter 40

Rita had rocked and cried on the private jet. When they'd landed on her private island, she'd rocked and cried in the Escalade that took them to the hilltop mansion. She'd even rocked and cried in bed until sleep embraced her hours later.

Now, sitting Indian-style on the white leather Versace sofa in Dr. Farr's office inside the Casa Casuarina, she rocked and cried again.

Dr. Melonie Farr was behind her desk. She too was crying. FBI agents had just left the mansion minutes prior with a load of confiscated computers and filing cabinets.

A helicopter buzzed around somewhere above the mansion.

"If I get arrested..." Rita didn't finish the sentence. She was far too upset to ponder such a notion.

"You'll be fine," Dr. Farr said. "It's Alexus who we have to worry about. She'll survive the shooting, but she may lose her life to the federal prison system the way they did Larry Hoover. He's got six life sentences."

"No." Rita shook her head. She wished it all was a dream. "Not my baby. They can't take my baby."

"Let's just pray that the surgeries are successful.

Think about the court stuff later. A good legal team can get her out of this, and Britney's firm is as good as they come."

Rita didn't know what to think. Her mind was running in a million different directions. Her entire body was trembling. "This can't be happening. This has to be a dream, Melonie. I thought the Costilla family had diplomatic immunity? What happened to all that mess?"

"The government is what happened," Dr. Farr said, and then she shut up, though she wanted to say more. She wasn't sure if the office was a safe place to talk. For all she knew the fed guys could have planted bugs all through the place during the raid. Too embarrassed to stand outside the mansion as an agent had ordered, she had sat in the Sprinter with Rita, the nanny, and the kids.

Dr. Farr dabbed at the tears that were running down her face.

Rita rocked back and forth, wishing Papi was alive at a time like this. He would've had the federal investigators dead and beheaded by now. Alexus wasn't strong enough to run such a mammoth drug operation at such young age. The system didn't fear her, so they were treating her with the same capitalistic punishments they had enforced on cartel bosses like Pablo Escobar and El Chapo.

"If only Alexus could channel a little of her father's determination into her right now," Rita murmured into a Kleenex tissue. "She'd overcome everything if only she took after her father just the tiniest bit."

"You're probably right," Farr said, regaining her composure. "Don't count her out just yet. I mean, we are talking about Alexus Costilla here. She's come out on top too many times to count her out now. Just pray about it. God can pull a person out of anything, especially a corporate titan like your daughter. She'll get found not guilty, the jurors will be set for life— you know how this'll go. Don't forget, we're in America. Money talks. Eighty-six billion dollars talks."

Rita nodded her head thoughtfully. She picked up her iPhone and tried to think of someone to call.

"No, Rita," Dr. Farr said. " Put that phone down. We both graduated from Harvard at the top of our classes." She took out a pen and pad. "Before we leave this office we'll have a master plan drawn out for Alexus and Costilla Corp. I'll get Britney on Skype."

Rita took a deep breath, nodding her head yes. She unfolded her meaty dark legs and crossed them professionally.

Months later in a Times magazine interview, she would tell of how God had suddenly taken over her during this session with Dr. Melonie Farr.

"It had to be God," she'd say. "There's no other explanation."

**Chapter 41

The cell was cold and remarkably clean. Blake was sitting up now, silent and shirtless. Every time he got arrested he never failed to implement a strict exercise regimen of sit-ups, push-ups, and lifting whatever was available to lift. Usually the latter consisted of large bags full of water or books.

He stood up, ready to begin a set of push-ups before his attorney visit.

Just then, Tattoo Face on the top bunk sat up and stared at him.

"Bulletface," was all the boy said.

Blake canted his head to the side and gave Tattoo a curious look. "Yeah, that's me? Erybody know me. You surprised or somethin'?"

"I'm Goldie. I was out there last night when shit popped off. Got pulled over tryna get away from that crazy ass shit." He looked at his fingernails and dug dirt from beneath them. "I know you heard them on the vent when I walked in."

"Yeah, I heard that fuck shit. Fuck them niggas. Matter of fact, watch this." He started toward the vent with the idea to yell down that he had $100,000 for somebody to smash on the Walkson brothers, but he stopped short and shook his head. "Never mind. Wait till I get back from seein' my lawyer. I'm on straight bullshit."

As if on cue, the intercom beeped at that very moment.

"King, attorney visit," an officer said.

Britney Bostic was always a stunning piece of eye candy when she decided to wear a dress and heels, and today was no different.

She wore a white dress that hugged her in all the right places over white Louboutin heels.

Blake entered the small visiting room grinning at her through the pane of glass that separated them. There was a waist-high table protruding from the glass with an opening over it that was wide enough to slide legal papers through. She had a white leather Birkin bag on the table, and she was drumming her fingernails on a stack of neatly stacked paperwork, smiling like it was just another day and not the end of the world for Blake and his wife.

"You'll get a bond at court today," she said, beaming. "It might be as high as $30 million but who cares, we'll get you right out. Alexus won't be eligible for bail until she's out of surgery and booked but we're probably looking at at least $100 million for her bond. That's if the judge doesn't consider her a flight risk. Just spoke with her doctors. She's in a coma. Can't talk or hear but she's breathing."

Blake gave a grateful nod and interlaced his fingers to give God a quick thanks.

"Did the feds hit the bread spot in California?" he asked.

Britney knew without question the "bread spot" he was speaking of. It was the Malibu megamansion where Alexus had over $150 billion in drug money hidden away.

The attorney's smile broadened at the mention of the Malibu mansion.

"Believe it or not, that's one of the only spots that hasn't been raided. Surprised me. I always thought they'd hit that place first if this ever happened." She shrugged. "Anyhow, I've got twelve lawyers and paralegals who will be going over your cases word for word. We're filing a lawsuit against the Michigan City Police Department for falsifying police reports as soon as you're out of court. I've received cell phone video of you surrendering, and at no time did you point a gun at those officers. I'll have their jobs for that alone and the charges will have to be dropped. Plus, there's no way your gun killed any of those people. If anything they should have charged you with unlawful use of a weapon. That's the only charge that would have had a chance of sticking. They have your guns. I'm pretty sure neither of them will come back as a murder weapon, but they're trying to say that one or more of your bullets killed Antoine McCullough."

"That's my nigga Batman."

"Yeah, well, Batman's dead."

Suddenly, Blake slammed his fist down on the

table.

He'd used his Mac-11 in the Haughville shooting.

"Settle down, Blake." Britney reached through the hole and squeezed his balled fist.

"We gotta get my guns back asap. I got a license to carry both of em."

"That will be impossible. They're evidence for now. The only thing important is getting you out of here. We can get the other stuff done later."

Blake let out a frustrated breath. He wanted Britney's hand to stay on his fist a little longer than it actually did. She pushed the arrest reports through to him.

"Feel free to read over those. Call me if you notice anything I haven't mentioned. If you're given a bond, you'll more than likely be released immediately after you get back from court. Don't go beating up on people like you did the last time you were here." She checked her rose gold Rolex watch for the time, then leaned forward and rested her elbows on the table. "You know how deep this all goes. There's something to those indictments. The fact that so many people close to Alexus haven't been named tells me that there's a plan I'm not seeing. And the indictments against Alexus are all hearsay really. Nothing solid. What I'm most surprised by is that Flako and Enrique's names weren't even mentioned. Enrique's already checked himself out of the hospital. I believe he's on his way to Mexico to reestablish control of the family business. I don't know." She bit the corner of her bottom lip. "Something's fishy."

"Just get me the fuck up outta here. I gotta be with Alexus."

"I hear you left upset shortly before the hotel bombing."

"Alexus be trippin'."

"So does Blake. Remember, I know you as much as I know her."

"Whatever." Blake fell back on the locked door behind him and rubbed a hand down his face. "Make sure Vari and King are safe. That's all I ask. And that Alexus is good. I don't care about nothing else."

The sound of the officer's keys jangling on his hip made Blake glance back over his shoulder.

The officer who'd brought him down to the visit was walking past with Brian Walkson.

Blake turned to face B-Walk and twisted the doorknob until his hand ached.

No use.

The door was locked.

"Calm down, Blake. Get back over here," Britney said.

B-Walk regarded Blake with a smirk and a head nod. "Sup, bro."

"Yeah, a'ight." Blake nodded too, only his was

replete with aggression.

He stared B-Walk down until they were no longer in sight.

When he turned back to Britney, he was almost furious.

"Get me the fuck outta here today," he snapped.

"I won't be able to do a thing if you show up to court with a new case."

"Whatever," he said again, because he was too angry to say anything else.

**Chapter 42

Tyrese Scott, sometimes known as Cup or Reesie or Red D, had been the sole owner of The Visionary Lounge, one of Chicago's most popular nightclubs, since it opened five years prior, and now he was making gains in the nightclub business by franchising and opening more TVLs all over the country. He currently had four more of them: one in Las Vegas, Nevada that had cost him $2.8 million to build and open; one in Seattle that had been a lot cheaper; one in Miami Beach that had run him $7.1 million; and another in Los Angeles, California that had cost him a whopping $12.8 million would have its grand opening at 10:00 pm tonight.

Relaxing in the backseat of his two-tone black and gold Bentley Mulsanne beside Shay Cooper, his slender-bodied assistant, while his driver, Lil Joe, accelerated the sleek quarter-million-dollar luxury vehicle through the elite city of Calabasas, Cup was biting down on a Cuban cigar and watching CNN on his computer tablet

The Costilla Cartel, his drug connect for more than eight years, had just been indicted.

"Just my luck," he complained selfishly. "How the fuck am I supposed to supply my city with the connects in the feds? If this ain't no bullshit, I don't know what is."

"You'll be fine." Shay's voice was as soft as

cotton. Cup loved hearing it. She put her hands on his shoulders and massaged them. "How about showing some excitement about tonight's grand opening. We've got Kendrick Lamar, Glasses Malone, and Keyshia Cole coming through to perform. You'll probably clear half a million on the first night of business."

"Yeah, but I'll lose millions more in the streets when I run out of work . Can't win for lose."

"Stop whining. You're rich already. Be content with what you have."

Cup shook off the suggestion and continued to watch CNN's live coverage of the "biggest drug bust in history." Apparently, federal authorities had seized over 100,000 kilos of cocaine from ten submarines off the coast of California, submarines the feds said belonged to the Costilla Cartel.

"See," Cup said, "if I had that much dope, I would stop hustling today. A hundred thousand bricks?!"

"Yeah, but what did you expect? It's Alexus Costilla being indicted. That's like if Bill Gates sold dope."

"Do you know her net worth? Her and Bulletface have $86 billion together. I see why he put a baby in that bad bitch. I would've. No question." He chuckled and slapped his knee. "It's okay, though. I got $50 million outta that bitch right when she inherited all them billions."

"I'd retire if I had that much money," Shay said wishfully. "The first thing I would do is pay somebody to get that fucker who killed my sister. Then I'd start a chain of clubs like you."

Shay's twin sister had been murdered by a Chicago gang member a couple of years ago. Cup had her sister's killer— a Vice Lord named Mikey who'd also made the near-fatal mistake of accepting a payment to kill Cup — shot up by one of his own friends, but Mikey had survived the shooting.

"You wouldn't retire," he said. "When I got $50 million I wanted $100 million. That's how it goes. It's why the rich are getting richer every year."

His smartphone rang as the Bentley was approaching the driveway to the Kardashian mansion.

He was here to make the Kardashian sisters an offer to make an appearance at his LA nightclub tonight.

But the phone call was from an Atlanta stripper he'd been trying to fuck for months, a bad yellowbone who went by the name Baddie Barbie.

He put his Kardashian visit on hold and answered the call.

****Chapter 43

"Hey, boo. Where you at?"

"Calabasas. Why, what's up?"

Twirling a lock of her pink-highlighted her around the tip of an index finger, Barbie swung her hips with every step as she sauntered through Lenox Square mall alongside her big sister.

They were headed to the Prada store.

The sight of them together— both wearing six-inch designer heels, revealing jeggings, diamond tennis bracelets, and black BMF shirts that exposed their belly button piercings— garnered the attention of just about every man and woman in the vicinity.

Barbie usually loved the attention.

Today she didn't much care for it.

The only thing on her mind was her sister's unsolved murder.

"I heard that nigga Bulletface got locked up for a body last night," she said into the phone. "You know anything about that?"

"Nah, not really. I saw he got arrested on the news. Ain't talked to him, though," Cup said. "I know he'll probably be out of there after court."

"So, you know him? Like, y'all are friends?"

Barbie eyed a maroon bag with a $2,100 price tag, while Fanny purchased a red one worth $700 more.

"I know that nigga. Why?"

"Just askin'."

"When you want me to slide on you?"

"Stop it, Cup. I told you, I don't do one night stands. Find you a lil Bankhead thot for that. They'll bust it open in the backseat for a pair of Nikes."

"Did I say anything about a one-night stand? I'm serious. What I gotta do?"

Tasia "Baddie Barbie" Olsen paused at another bag. She gazed vacantly at the elaborate design, thinking not of fashion but of vengeance and murder.

A strange-looking dark-skinned man with red dreadlocks and skinny jeans walked up beside her and looked at the maroon bag she'd just been eyeing.

Finally she said, "Introduce me to Bulletface as soon as he bonds out. Do that and I'll give you what you want."

"Yeah?"

"Yeah." She said it gently, stretching the word out."

"I can do that."

"You can't tell him anything about me and you. Just tell him my Instagram name. He knows me. He liked one of my pictures yesterday."

"I want a whole night for this shit."

"You got it, daddy. Let me go, I'll talk to you later. Thank you so much. You won't regret it."

"Send me a video or somethin' until then. Lemme see what I'm gettin'."

"I'll post a video on IG."

"Nah."

"Take it or leave it."

He laughed. "A'ight then, lil mama. I'll hit you up later."

A conspiratorial smile appeared on Barbie's perfect face.

The man with the red dreadlocks must have thought she was smiling at him.

"Hey, cutie," he said, stroking his goatee. He had on one of those leather Young Thug skirts, and she noticed his fingernails were painted red.

"Kick rocks, nigga," Barbie replied, and headed off to find her sister.

****Chapter 44

Blake was fuming when he made it back to the cell block. As soon as the dayroom door slammed shut behind him, he said, "If any one of you niggas fuck wit' V-Walk or B-Walk you's a hoe-ass nigga and we can throw these hands right now, nigga!"

He didn't know what to expect, so when a short, cocky guy with crooked teeth and the ugliest face Blake had seen in a long while got up from one of the tables and stuck his chest out aggressively, Blake took a few seconds to react.

"You ain't gon' be disrespectin' my Folks. Ain't nobody in here disrespectin' yo' Lords."

Remo said, "Sit down somewhere, Pee Wee. I've been in here with Blake before. You don't wanna get in no fight with this man, I'm tellin' you what I know."

But it was too late.

Blake was already storming off toward his cell, snatching off his striped jail shirt and signaling Pee Wee to join him.

Entering the cell, he glimpsed Goldie lying with his head at the vent.

Then Pee Wee walked in, and Blake rushed him.

Anticipating a brawl, Blake let Pee Wee swing first. It was a wild punch that Blake had no problem dodging before landing a vicious three-piece combo to the ugly, bumpy face.

Pee Wee was knocked out before he hit the floor. The back of his head struck the steel toilet and started bleeding.

Goldie got up and out of the way.

"Bitch ass nigga!" Blake snapped, leaning down to scream in the vent. "I got a hundred bands for any nigga down there to pumpkin head them hoe ass niggas B-Walk and V-Walk! Bulletface said that!"

He was turning back to Pee Wee when he was suddenly punched several times in the face...by Goldie.

"You want smoke wit' my family?!" the gold-mouthed thug shouted.

Stumbling aside, Blake shifted toward his attacker and threw a powerful haymaker. His fist struck Goldie's mouth. A glimmer of gold flew out from between Goldie's lips as they began exchanging blows.

Goldie was quick, but Blake was stronger, his punches much more damaging. Soon he had the scrawny teen on the floor in the rear of the cell, punching and kicking him until he was out cold like Pee Wee. Old school Remo tried grabbing Blake and caught an elbow to the face.

Finally, Blake stopped and looked around the

room.

There was blood everywhere.

Rico G was at the door, looking around with a shocked expression on his long brown face.

Remo was leaving the cell with a hand on his jaw.

"Now," Blake said, "who else want some? Anybody else rockin' wit' them niggas?"

A deep voice boomed through the vent:

"You're a dead man, Blake! On my dead brother."

"Nah," Blake replied. "You fuck niggas gon' join that nigga in the grave. Let me catch you pussies on the streets. I'm on that."

**Chapter 45

Enrique's nephew, Sergio Aleman, was a portly 17-year-old Mexican boy with an insatiable appetite for Doritos, Snickers bars, Little Debbie cakes, and M&M's. He was one of the only bodyguards that didn't meet the physical requirements, but Rita didn't mind having him around. No matter how many cakes and candies he ate, he was always on his job.

Rita was up on her feet, pacing back and forth in front of Dr. Farr's desk with a cup of Starbucks in hand, spouting out ideas to add to the ones on Farr's notepad, when Sergio knocked on the door and peeked his head in.

"Rita, can I get you for a second?"

"Can it wait?"

"Afraid it can't."

With a reluctant sigh and a despondent shake of the head, Rita told Dr. Farr that she'd be right back and stepped out in the hallway with Enrique's corpulent nephew just as Vari and King Neal were racing by behind him in their miniature Range Rovers.

"Well," he said, and dumped a bunch of peanut M&M's in his mouth, "to keep it short" —he took a brief talking break to chew and swallow— "I just got a call from my uncle. He's in bad shape. Lost his left hand. He thinks he may know who the vato was that gave that girl the bomb. It's the fucking ISIS bastard —"

"Watch your mouth," Rita scolded.

"Sorry about that. What I'm saying is that this guy's a serious threat. Enrique wants you to leave the country."

"As long as my daughter's here, I'll be here."

Rita turned to go back into Farr's office; Sergio grabbed her wrist.

"Think about this, Rita. I mean seriously think about it. You remember how evil Jenny Costilla was. They say this guy makes her look like a petty thief."

"No one can make Jenny look like a petty thief. She blew up Washington DC and half of Mexico with nuclear weapons. Never in history has there been a more dangerous terrorist than Jenny."

Sergio made a clicking sound with his mouth and waved an index finger from left to right, left to right. "There's something you may not know about Juan Costilla — the younger one, I mean, the terrorist, not Alexus's dad." He emptied the rest of his M&M's in his hungry mouth and crumpled the wrapper in his fist. "You see, Jenny went to a terrorist training camp in Syria back in 1999, way before most of us became aware of the dangers Middle-Eastern terrorist groups like Al Qaeda and

ISIS would pose to us in the future. That's how Jenny became so ruthless. She learned from the most ruthless Al Qaeda instructor there was. His name then was Hassan Naseer, but his real name was and always has been Juan Costilla."

The fear registered immediately in Rita, though she did her best to keep her expression indecipherable.

She couldn't believe it.

The man who'd nearly succeeded in killing her daughter was the same man who trained the world's most dangerous terrorist.

"He couldn't have gotten here to Miami by now, could he?" she murmured, more to herself than to Sergio.

"No. Definitely not. He's laying low. Feds are all over Indianapolis searching for him. Enrique thinks he's still in the country somewhere, just biding his time until his next attack. He won't stop until everyone with the last name Costilla is dead."

When Rita returned to Dr. Farr's office, she was a lot paler than she'd been before the talk with Sergio.

Farr noticed. "What's wrong, Rita?"

"What isn't."

"Wanna talk about it?"

"Not now."

"Back to the notes?"

"Yes."

****Chapter 46

Five minutes after Blake demolished Pee Wee and Goldie the same officer who'd brought him to the cell block and took him to and from his attorney visit came back to get him and Remo out for court.

They ate lunch downstairs in the "bullpen", the cell he'd been in when he first got to the jail, and then they were handcuffed and shackled and led out to two waiting vans, one for female inmates, and the other for them.

Blake intended to mind his business and remain silent until he saw his lawyer but Remo's black ass got the seat right next to him, and as always the old man had a million things to say.

"You know you 'bout broke my damn jaw elbowin' me like that," he said, raising his hands to rub the side of his face. "Don't know why you beat on them po' boys like that knowin' the lil niggas couldn't fight. You could've just played wit' em. Didn't have to do em like that."

Blake shook his head and kept quiet.

"I know ya fixin' to bond out. Might as well get me out wit'cha. 'Fore dey send me to the joint. Got four years backup. It'd be nice to see my family for a li'l summer before I go down."

Blake leaned his head to the side and stared at the old guy for a couple of seconds.

"What?" Remo said. "My bond ain't shit. Ain't even a thousand dollars. Eight hundred. You probably spend that kinda money partyin' every night."

"You talk alotta shit for a old man," Blake said.

Remo found this funny; he laughed until tears gathered in the corners of his eyes. Blake didn't believe it was as funny as Remo was making it seem. He thought the old guy was running game, and the laugh was just a part of it.

"Miss me wit' that bullshit, nigga. Shit ain't that muhfuckin funny."

"It is. I talk good shit, young nigga. You need to pay attention. Why don't you gimme one of them millionaire jobs so I can get these people off my back? That's the only reason a nigga can't duck the joint. Ain't no jobs. Damn right I'm gon' rob and sell dope if I can't get a job. A nigga gotta eat."

Blake looked out the two windows in the van's rear doors. They were just crossing the highway, leaving LaPorte and entering Michigan City. He'd taken this court ride a dozen times.

"I'll get you out," he said. "I'll give you a job, too. Fuck up one time and it's over, though."

"What's that supposed to mean?"

"Just what it sounded like."

This preceded more humorous requests from the other five prisoners on the van (one of them, a skinny white kid with thick-lensed glasses, promised to get his "hot chick" to pay the $2,500 back in "gold or hole", which elicited a laugh from everyone), and Blake decided to bond them all out. He remembered once being in the county jail with a $1,500 bond that his family took weeks to pay. It felt good to be able to pay it forward.

There were four black Rolls-Royce Phantoms parked in the lot next to the courthouse when the big brown jail vans arrived. Blake spotted Donna's van and for a second he was glad that Alexus wasn't here.

Then he thought of her condition and felt bad for the idea.

Three officers with guns on their hips led them in via the courthouse's side door and into a holding room. Before Blake could sit Britney Bostic was at the door to get him.

She took him to a room across the hall amid shouts of "Don't forget us" and "Fuck them, just come back for me." He was laughing when he sat down on the other side of a long wooden table from Britney.

"What are they screaming about?" she asked, displaying the beaming smile that she was known for and shuffling through some papers.

"Never mind them, what's up wit' me?"

The stunning black woman in white's Colgate smile broadened. "Tell me I'm the best first."

"I'll tell you that after you tell me I'm goin' home."

Blake said drably.

"The shooting cases were dropped, and I showed the prosecutor evidence that you never aimed a gun at anyone. They had no choice but to drop all charges. All you'll do in court is show your face and hear that the charges have been dropped. You'll go back to jail to get your belongings and then you're a free man."

Blake's spirits rose quickly. "Where is Biggs?"

"Still in the hospital. We'll get him flown out to LAX later tonight. First we have to get you out of here. I assume you want your jet ready for takeoff. Young Meach, Scrill, and Mocha are all here. So is some girl named Dominique who claims to have a bag you left over her place. You'll see them all in court."

A winning grin stretched across Blake's face. The money was nothing to him, but he hadn't expected Dominique and her mother to keep it a hundred with his duffle bag. He figured they'd be on the highway somewhere by now, fleeing toward a new life with $500,000 cash.

He was in and out of the courtroom in minutes.

An hour later he was in the passenger seat of Meach's Phantom, smoking Kush and sipping Lean on the highway en route to O'Hare International Airport, where his private jet was gassed up and waiting to fly them all to Los Angeles to be with Alexus."

Remo was two car-lengths behind them in the

white Bugatti.

"These fuck niggas can't stop me," Blake said, grinning at his reflection in the visor mirror. He studied his teardrop tattoos, remembering every murder he'd committed in his beef with Trintino Walkson; he eyed the three old bullet wounds in his face and thought of how blessed he was to have survived them. "I'm the king out here, li'l bruh. A god to these niggas. Ain't none of the big homies in the rap game even fuckin' wit' me no more. I am the big homie. The streets fuck wit' me tough. The niggas in the joint fuck wit' me tough. And niggas know it's salute me or shoot me."

"Bruh, you a fool. Awready, though." Meach laughed. He too was sipping Lean as he traversed the congested Interstate-94. "We Money Bagz, nigga. Big 4's, big T's. Solid world. Ain't nobody stoppin' us. We da bad guys. Fuck em if they ain't on our side."

"On Dub Life," Blake said.

Already he had another gun — a black Glock 27 with red laser sighting and a 30-round clip— on his lap.

He couldn't wait to use it.

****Chapter 47

"...And last but not least, Grammy-nominated rapper Bulletface has been released from jail after all charges were dismissed following a northern Indiana shooting that claimed the lives of four and wounded thirty more. As it turns out, police officers witnessed the beginnings of an argument between Bulletface and two others. The two men— famed

TV producer Trintino Walkson's brothers— allegedly opened fire on Bulletface, who then returned fire, resulting in Bulletface's arrest. However, it's now been proved that his gun was not the murder weapon.

"Bulletface's long-standing beef with T-Walk has been the source of numerous documentaries on the Midwest's endless stream of gang wars. T-Walk, whose death is still an unsolved case, is rumored to have met up with Bulletface at a Miami strip club shortly before the rapper was gunned down late last year.

"T-Walk was murdered two days later by an unknown gunman. With that in mind, this Indiana shooting doesn't seem so shocking. Bulletface fans are saying that they were waiting for something like this to go down in the same way the Hip Hop community expected Biggie's death to follow Tupac's. It is a war that has led to hundreds of murders throughout the Midwest, mostly between

Gangster Disciples— which T-Walk was— and the faction of Vice Lords that Bulletface has been tied to for years..."

Blake's winning grin was still present on his Gulfstream 650 private jet and all the way to LAX. With close to $300,000 on the table in front of him (he'd given Donna and Dominique $200,000 to split for the damages to their apartment and the beginning of a new life), he was reclined in his white leather and Louis Vuitton seat on the jet long after it landed, smoking Kush and sipping from his Styrofoams, watching TMZ Live as Harvey and Charles talked about him.

"It's not good to always be in the news for shootings," Mocha said as she sashayed past his seat in a black leather miniskirt under a skimpy MBM t-shirt with a picture of Blake and Young Meach in front and pics of Will Scrill and her on the sides. "R.I.P. Pat, Yellowboy, Lil Mike, and Young D" was scribbled in cursive in red thread across one shoulder. Her studded Giuseppe Zanotti heels lifted her up to 5'10". She dropped down into the seat across from him and popped open a bottle of Ace of Spades.

Meach and Scrill were shooting dice in the aisle, their long gold and diamond chains and MBM pendants swinging from their necks, piles of bank-new Benjamins in their hands. Meach was down $80,000, and while rolling he was reminiscing about last night when he'd won $145,000 from Wale and Rick Ross backstage at an MMG/MBM concert in Atlanta.

"Sh-She right, bruh," Meach said. Sometimes he stuttered. The only time he was stutter-free was in the studio. "All that sh-shootin' gotta stop. Look at you, bruh. L-Look at us. We on top. Beef is a broke man's sport."

"I'm chillin'. I ain't got no beef." Blake leaned over the side of his seat and showed an icy grin that said otherwise. "Nigga, do I look like I'm worried about some beef? I'm servin' niggas mad cow disease if they want beef. Y'all know dat shit like they know it."

"Just chill, bruh," Scrill said, agreeing with Meach. "It's all about gettin' money. Fuck that hatin' shit. That's all killin' is hate. We about life, bruh. We're artists. We do this shit for our fans and in return they give us their money for albums and shows. That's all to it. We ain't no hoe ass rats or no police ass niggas. Muhfuckas know dat. We ain't got nothin' to prove."

Mocha sucked her teeth and took a gulp of Ace straight from the bottle. "Blake is not going to listen to either of us," she said, biting the corner of her bottom lip and staring at him. "He's like a black Scarface for real. He was a cold-hearted fucker before he was a billionaire. Now's he's just more ruthless because of the money. I can't believe I've made you over a hundred and seventy million dollars and all I've gotten is $22.4 million."

"You didn't have that before we met!" Blake

snapped. But he calmed quickly and grinned. "We're family, Mocha. All this money is family money. Whatever you want I give you. Say I don't? You gotta work for this bread, though. Work for it like I worked. You'll enjoy it more. And think of how many bitches you know that done had $22.4 million. Name one you went to school wit'. Name one from the hood you grew up in. Don't worry, I'll wait."

Young Meach cracked up laughing. "Damn, M-Mocha. He just hitchoo with the Katt Williams."

Will Scrill laughed, too.

Mocha flipped Blake a middle finger, but she couldn't help joining in the laughter.

He laughed with her.

In his mind, he thought of how close of a call this had really been. Mocha was making him millions hand over fist. Having her unhappy wasn't good at all.

He changed the subject to Cup, who'd been texting him since he got his smartphone back as he left the county jail.

"The nigga say he got a bad bitch for me," Blake said, more to Meach and Scrill than to Mocha.

"Yeah?" said Scrill. "That why you got us waiting on this plane for so long?"

"Nah. They say I can't visit Alexus until 8:30. We got like three hours till then. Cup said the bitch flying in now. We'll leave when she gets here. I saw the bitch the other day. She's a stripper named Baddie Barbie."

"Just saw her at my show in Atlanta," Meach said. "She baaaaaaad, bruh. Face like Keyshia Cole, body like Maliah. Dumb thick, on Angelo."

Scrill shook his head. "You gon' fuck a new bitch when you got wifey in the hospital facin' federal indictments?"

Blake took a brief moment to ponder his reply; then, "I know it's fucked up. I need some pussy tonight, though. I don't care. Gotta stop lovin' these hoes 'cause they ain't lovin' me. She pulled a gun on me again. I can't keep goin' for that. She gon' make me kill her muhfuckin ass if she don't serve the rest of her life for that drug sweep. They just hit her people wit' a hundred thousand bricks. We need to be blowin' money fast before we hit that feds list, nigga. I'm at the dealership first thing tomorrow wit' a bad bitch and a new Bugatti."

"Can't knock you, bruh," Meach said, a second before he cracked Scrill for $10,000 on a side bet. "Bad bitches are here for real niggas. You supposed to hit that shit and quit that shit. You got a billion by yourself. The world is yours. Enjoy that shit."

Blake couldn't knock himself. He was a famous rap star, the richest rapper in the game now. With his marriage to Alexus, he was the richest black man alive.

He felt that, considering the circumstances, he deserved a new bad bitch to enjoy himself while his wife was in the hospital...and probably on her way to prison for the rest of her life.

I wonder why they didn't indict me, he thought to himself.

But it wasn't a long thought.

Just then, Cup's Bentley pulled up alongside the private jet and parked at the end of the extended staircase.

Blake saw them from his window. He got up, dumped the cash and his gun in the duffle, and carried it out to the top of the stairs to meet the steatopygic young Atlanta dancer.

He watched her every move as she gingerly put one Louis Vuitton heel out and then the other. Luscious yellowish-brown legs exposed by the slit in a brown Louis Vuitton dress came next.

Then she was out of the Mulsanne, sauntering past the trio of black Rolls-Royces and Blake's white Bugatti as if approaching the stripper pole. She wore dark sunglasses, a host of diamond jewelry, what seemed to be just the slightest amount of makeup, and the standard Michael Kors bag hanging under an arm.

Blake walked down the stairs to her, ogling her amazing curves and flawless complexion.

"Take them glasses off," he said when he made it to her.

She stopped, took off the sunglasses, and put her

hands on her hips. Her eyes scanned him from head to toe, and it was funny to Blake; it was what Alexus had done to him the first day they met.

"Damn, you look familiar," he said, though he knew the Lean and Kush in his system would make it an impossibility to remember who exactly it was she reminded him of.

"You cute or whatever," she said with a half-smile.

She got in the backseat of the four-door Bugatti with him, and Remo, his old friend and new driver, followed the Rolls-Royces to Blake and his wife's ninety-million-dollar Beverly Hills mansion.

****Chapter 48

Enrique was nobody's dummy. He'd been a loyal member of the Costilla Cartel going on 20 years. Every time there had ever been a drug bust or an indictment list, every person in the top boss's circle went down with them.

But this time was different.

Enrique wasn't on the list.

Flako Costilla wasn't on the list.

Blake wasn't on the list.

Not even the crooked FBI agent, Josh Sneed, was on the list.

It seemed like someone was meticulously picking off certain members of the cartel while leaving others in play.

Enrique had a pretty good idea of who the man behind it all was.

Which is why he was in a wheelchair being pushed through a massive marble-floored palace in Juarez, Mexico that Flako Costilla had paid close to $100 million in drug money to have built from the ground up.

There were armed men everywhere, AK-47-toting Mexican men with masks on their faces and bullet-resistant vests on over their camouflage uniforms.

Many of them were ex Los Zetas and Sinaloa cartel members.

All of them knew Enrique. He was considered a top boss of the Costilla Cartel since he was so close to Alexus Costilla.

The armed men paid little attention to Enrique.

The girl pushing him was named Selena Laredo, though Enrique wasn't sure if it was the name given to her at birth. He'd known her since his early days as a Costilla Cartel assassin in the late 90's. He often visited her during his rare trips away from Alexus, and he suspected that her two daughters were his, but his connection to so many of Mexico's most deadly drug cartels kept him from wanting to find out for certain. Still, he sent her $50,000-a-month to take care of them, and he never forgot to phone them on their birthdays.

He directed her to an elevator that was made of 24-karat gold, and he didn't speak until they were alone inside it.

"Give it to me," he said, staring at the gauze-wrapped stomp where his left hand had been before the Indianapolis hotel blast. It peeked out from the sleeve of his finely tailored black Hartmarx suit.

Selena dug in her bra and pulled out a gold-plated .38 Special with Enrique's name etched along its left side. He took it in his only hand and placed it beneath the Louis Vuitton scarf that covered his lap.

"Whatever happens, don't panic," he said. "Just remain calm. We'll get through this."

"This isn't my first rodeo through Juarez," she replied.

"I understand that. But these guys are dangerous."

"I'll be fine, Enrique. Just go in there and talk to him. It can't be that difficult. See what's going on with them and go on from there."

The elevator came to an abrupt stop on the third floor.

Selena wheeled him down a hallway lined with even more armed men. She stopped at the big gold door at the end of the hall and knocked.

"Come on in, my friend," Flako bellowed from inside the room.

Selena turned the knob and swung the door open.

Keeping his eyes on Flako, who was sitting at his big oak desk with an open kilo of cocaine and a bottle of expensive cognac set out in front of him, Enrique took several deep breaths, wincing at the vibrating pain of his fresh burns, and tried to think of all the possible ways this could turn out.

Behind Flako's desk was a waist-high bed of cash, rubber-banded bundles of what looked to be all hundred-dollar bills. On top of it lay a buxom Latina in a white Gucci bikini and an arsenal of assault rifles and handguns that were all custom designed in diamonds and gold.

One of the gaudy handguns— a .50-caliber Desert Eagle — was in his left hand.

Selena parked Enrique's wheelchair in front of Flako's desk and stepped back out to the hallway.

"They're arresting everybody!" Flako said, and slammed his fist on the desk so hard his bottle of liquor bounced. "It's an in-house job. I'm telling you, there's no way the feds figured everything out on their own. Somebody's in on this! You hear me? Somebody's in on this and I'm going to have their goddamned heads for it!"

He snorted from a pile of cocaine and then looked at Enrique as if just realizing he had company.

"Oh. Oh. The bombing. Jesus, what happened?"

"It was Juan."

"I've said it once and I'll say it twice, that fucker is going down real fucking soon."

"I'll take care of him."

"How's the queen?"

"She'll live."

"It's crazy, I tell you." A sardonic smile grew from the fat man's scowl. "On second thought, it might not be so bad. I mean, yeah, they got Alexus, they got Pedro, and all the other bosses, but at least I'm still around. I mean, at least we've got me. And you. And that FBI agent. I see Blake made it out of that little situation he got himself into. We can still do some things. We've got ten more submarines and fourteen underground tunnels. The Colombians weren't indicted. We can use Blake's street connections to help move the dope faster. They haven't stopped us. Nobody can stop the fucking Costilla Cartel. Screw those federal assholes. The show will go on, no matter how many of us they arrest. They took down all of the bosses, but they forgot about me! I'm still here! Fuckers."

"Well," Enrique said, "technically you're not the boss if we lose Alexus."

Flako's jovial expression became frozen. He stared at Enrique, waiting for an explanation. His nostrils were called full of coke. His blue Hartmarx suit and tie had sprinkles of cocaine all over its upper half. He was like a Pablo Escobar lookalike, an overweight drug boss with way too much money and power. His thick mustache seemed to mock him every time he spoke.

"I'd have to be in charge of things," Flako said, his tone uncertain. "I'm the only boss left with Pedro gone and Alexus in the hospital."

"No." Enrique shook his head.

"What do you mean no!" His hand pounded the desk again.

"Alexus is the boss of all bosses," Enrique explained. "She's married. If she's not able to run things, her husband must take charge. Just as Vida Costilla did when Segovia was killed."

Stone-faced, Flako eased back in his chair and stared at Enrique for a very long moment. Cocaine crumbs fell from his nose. When he finally spoke, it was in a rage.

"We can't have a fucking nigger running a Mexican drug cartel! Are you out of your fucking mind! This is the Costilla Cartel! The Costilla Cartel! I will not sit on my ass while some goddamned rap star runs the business that my ancestors have fought and bled for! Over my dead body!"

"So be it," Enrique said, and in one swift sweep of the hand he raised the revolver and shot Flako square on the nose.

The woman lying on the pile of money screamed.

The next bullet Enrique fired hit her in the left ear as she attempted to sit up.

Enrique's hand was weaponless and held high in surrender when Flako's armed men stormed the room.

He'd tossed the gun and raised his smartphone.

"Alexus's orders!" Enrique shouted repeatedly. He made his voice as authoritative and stern as possible. "She's in an American hospital. Her husband's in charge now. Shall I call him for our next orders?"

****Chapter 49

Blake sat in the Jacuzzi with his Styrofoams in his left hand and a blunt of Blue Dream Kush pinched between the thumb and forefinger of his right hand. He had on a combination of black and white diamond jewelry and black Versace boxers.

Mocha was on his left, steadily swallowing down mouthfuls of Ace and rolling blunts for Blake to fire up.

To his right was Barbie. Or Baddie Barbie. He wasn't sure which name she preferred. All he knew was that she was as thick as Free from the old 106th and Park in her one-piece Louis Vuitton swimsuit and he was glad to have the yellowbone stripper's perfectly manicured fingertips rubbing up and down the rippling muscles of his dark hued chest, while her tongue pranced on the side of his neck and made his dick stand like a soldier at attention.

Biggs and his sister Nona had just arrived. The wound to his thigh had only been a graze, but the other shot had broken his arm, and now it was in a cast and a sling. He was seated next to Nona in one of the many white leather chairs that lined the back wall.

The dice game Meach and Scrill started on the private jet had moved to the white-and-gold marble floor in front of the 110-inch Samsung Ultra HDTV that hung on the wall across from the 20-seat

Jacuzzi.

The movie playing on the television was Scarface.

Barbie's hand slipped into Blake's boxers just as the iPhone 6 on the floor behind him rang.

He reached back and picked it up. "Enrique," he said when he saw the number.

He answered the call.

"What's up, Rique?"

"You're the top boss of the family business," Enrique said. "At least until Alexus is back. We have a shipment on the way from Colombia first thing tomorrow. A hundred thousand t-shirts. The only workers we lost are the ones Flako knew about. He turned everyone over to the feds, tried to make a power move but it backfired. Now you're the boss."

Barbie had his dick out of the costly boxers, squeezing and stroking it underwater.

On the TV, Tony Montana was quitting his low-wage job to deal drugs.

After so many indictments, the phone conversation had Blake paranoid.

Enrique must have read his mind.

"You know these things have signal scramblers. No need to worry over who's listening."

Blake chuckled. "I was thinking that."

"I know," Enrique said. "There will be somewhere

in the neighborhood of twenty thousand t-shirts left over after we dump the rest on our La Eme friends, in case you want to make a few moves yourself."

"Yep. I'm busy now. I'll hit you —"

"You're not busy," Enrique interrupted. "You're at the Beverly Hills mansion. I had a drone follow you from LAX, and you have forty-three heavily-armed soldiers all within five blocks from you in case you need assistance. They'll be with you until you leave California. And don't worry, what Alexus doesn't know won't hurt her."

Enrique ended the call abruptly, leaving Blake sitting there with his mouth wide open.

It wasn't the fact that he'd been followed that had him in such a state of bewilderment.

It was the realization that he was now in charge of the Costilla Cartel, the most powerful and wealthy drug organization in all of Mexico.

****Chapter 50

Porsche was upset over Mercedes being in the hospital, but at least her plan was beginning to come together.

There were over two hundred Black Disciples gathered in front of the Parkway Gardens buildings on 64th and Calumet. Glo was at the forefront of the crowd, relaying to them the message that his loyal woman had pounded into his head.

Porsche was watching from inside her Range Rover, which was parked behind a Doritos delivery truck at the curb in front of Parkway Hoagies.

Seated next to her was Sasha.

She was eating the other half of Porsche's corned beef sandwich. The two of them had quickly become friends after the day of Gerome Hoover's murder, and they'd been hanging out ever since.

She'd taken Sasha on a $10,000 shopping spree (which explained the Prada shoes and Gucci outfit Sasha now wore) and given her $5,000 to hold on to. Sasha hadn't held on to much of it. After buying a used minivan for her parents and giving her hospitalized brother a grand, Sasha had little left for herself. Porsche didn't mind that her new friend hadn't saved the money. She planned on giving Sasha a few more grand just because. She needed a down ass friend to hang out with since her big sister had abandoned her for Alexus, and keeping her new friend classy and well-maintained was a must.

"So," Sasha asked, "they're gonna just pop up at Bulletface's shows and start demanding money? I cannot wait to see that shit on Facebook. They thought it was something when Fat Ass had the GD's on him, I know bitches are going to lose it when they see some niggas extorting Bulletface."

Porsche turned to her window and stared out at Glo and his gang of young savages. Her mind was on Bulletface, the man whose love she wanted but knew she'd never get. She wondered what he was doing now, and if he ever thought of her as much as she thought of him. Deep down she hated going against him. She really had nothing against him.

Her beef was with Alexus.

"That hoe got me shot. She had my momma killed, too," she muttered.

"What?" said Sasha.

"I'm talking about Alexus," Porsche explained. "She thought Blake was cheating on her with some girl named Whitney, so her men went out and killed a bunch of women with the name Whitney. To get back at Blake. My momma was innocent, didn't even know Blake. The killer knocked on her door and asked for Whitney. When she told him she was Whitney, he shot her and drove away."

"Oh, my God, are you serious? That's so fucked up."

"I know, right? And now that bitch is the richest

person in the world. Now she got my sister laying in the hospital with her 'cause she done made some damn terrorist mad. It ain't fair. You know it ain't fair." Porsche tried to hold back the tears but they came anyway. She soaked them up with a napkin.

"It sure ain't," Sasha agreed, shaking her head and stuffing the last of the sandwich in her mouth. She chewed and swallowed. "Fucked up part is, she sent some niggas to try to off you for fucking her man, when she's really the bogus bitch for having your mom killed. It's a shame too 'cause I looked up to that bitch. Fuck her, too. We can ride on them opp hoes."

Porsche laughed at Sasha's ride-or-die attitude. She was always talking about riding on some "opp hoes".

A couple of minutes later Glo got in the backseat and told Porsche to pull off.

"Lil folks n'em ready." He slid two Glocks from under his GBE hoody and set them down on his lap. "Next time that nigga Bulletface do a show out here we on his ass. He got a concert with T.I. and Lil Wayne scheduled for April twenty-first at Soldier Field and the after party supposed to be at Adrianna's. I'm gon' have the lil folks air his tour bus out if he don't come with that bread. We need a quarter million off top."

"I wish we could make Alexus pay," Porsche said.

"If Bulletface paying you might as well say she paying. That's his wife, ain't it?" Glo said as he rolled a blunt of loud. "That nigga just got out of jail. Don't even worry, baby. We on his ass. Next time he steps foot in Chiraq, he gon' pay or we on straight drills. No talk."

Porsche hit the highway and headed out west, bumping some Katie Got Bandz and Lil Durk while Glo watched a 4Ever Bunz porn on the televisions behind the headrests. She wished she could somehow make Alexus pay with her life instead of with cash. The bullet wound in her shoulder was healing, but it still hurt like hell, and every time the wound ached she thought of Alexus.

'At least I'm doing something to the bitch', she thought. 'Something is better than nothing. I'll be a needle in that bitch's side until the day I die, and that's if I don't kill her first.'

**Chapter 51

Ushering Barbie to the master bedroom, Blake tried to focus solely on what he was about to do to her and not on what he would have to do as the Costilla Cartel's newest leader.

He wanted to tell someone, but then again he didn't. Maybe it was better to keep it to himself. If people found out that he was responsible for 95% of America's cocaine he knew what would happen. He'd be stuck somewhere in a federal prison like Big Meech, and that was an outcome that he truly wanted to avoid.

There was a white leather sofa at the foot of the king size bed. His Louis Vuitton duffle bag was on it, as well as Barbie's Michael Kors bag. They had put them here before going to the Jacuzzi.

He pushed down and kicked off his soggy boxers and then dug in the duffle for the box of Magnum condoms he'd purchased in Michigan City.

He sat down on the sofa, still awestruck over his sudden rise to power.

Barbie kneeled down between his parted thighs and began squeezing and shaking his dick in both hands.

"I won't walk right for a year if you know how to use this big ass thing." She spit on the topside of it and stroked his length a couple of times before sucking it into her mouth.

"I know how to use it," Blake said, putting a hand on the back of Barbie's head and forcing himself to the back of her throat.

He thrust his hips upward, fucking her throat and biting his bottom lip as he looked at her beautiful face. He wondered how many dicks she'd sucked during her time as a stripper and came to the conclusion that it must have been many. She was much too good at it.

Following a few minutes of intense sucking, she stood up and did a little dance for him, making her ass clap, jiggle, bounce, and jump.

"Look at all this ass, nigga," she said, her tone replete with arrogance. She slapped her hands on her ass and spread the big yellow cheeks apart. "Alexus ain't even got ass like this. This that Tay—that Barbie, I mean."

Blake was tearing open a condom when he caught the stutter. "What was that name you just said? You said Tay? That's your real name."

She turned to face him. "No, nigga." She planted her hands on her hips. "I was about to say my friend's name. My girl Tay who works at Onyx with me. Then I remembered you don't know her."

"You so fuckin' bad."

"I am, ain't I?"

"If that pussy good I'm takin' you shoppin' all week. A hun'ed bands-a-day. Might blow a million on you."

"You gon' wanna blow more than a million."

"Yeah?" He rolled the rubber down his twelve-inch pole.

"Yeah." Barbie took off her swimsuit and bent over on the sofa just as a Tamar Braxton ringtone began chiming in her purse.

She ignored the call.

Blake wasted no time in getting behind Barbie and cramming his dick deep inside her.

The snugness of her vaginal walls felt so good that

he closed his eyes immediately and took a moment to enjoy the feel of her tightly gripping juice box.

"Pull my hair," she said, so he wrapped her long hair around his fist and pulled her head back as he began fucking her mercilessly.

They moved from the sofa to the floor, and he held her knees up and slammed in and out of her while she moaned and clawed at his back; then to the gold-framed window, where he stood her up and pounded her from the back; and finally to the bed, where Barbie put her head down and her ass up and gazed back at Blake, making the sexiest of sex faces climaxing twice in a row before watching him yank off the condom and send five ribbons of semen

jetting down onto her bountiful derrière.

Blake grinned, slapping his deflating phallus on her ass as shook she shook and bounced it.

"Best pussy you ever had," she said with a weak laugh.

Her phone started ringing again.

She got up and took the smartphone out of her purse. "Let me get this, it's my sister."

"Do you," Blake said.

She grabbed the purse and put the phone to her ear as she walked into the bathroom with cum dripping down between her thighs.

Blake grabbed his own smartphone and fell back on the bed. He still had an hour before he could see his wife, and he was going to spend at least twenty more minutes with the stripper.

As bad as Barbie was, he didn't rule out spending the entire hour with her.

He went to Instagram to look at her page, but the phone rang with another call from Enrique before he could reach out.

"I forgot to tell you something," Enrique said. "Before the blast, Alexus was going to call and warn you about somebody. It was important. Somebody asking questions about that Tasia and Tee Tee situation."

"Who was askin' questions?"

"That's the thing. I don't know. Alexus and Mercedes were talking about it, and Alexus dialed your number to tell you. Then that girl ran over and exploded. Just keep an eye open. We'll figure it out.

Talk to you later."

Blake set the phone aside and interlaced his fingers behind his head. He stared up at the ceiling with a quizzical look on his face.

Who had Alexus felt the need to warm him about?

With the phone trapped between her shoulder and ear, Barbie locked the door, put her purse on the sink, and pushed her hand down to the very bottom of it to make sure her pearl-handled .25-caliber handgun was still there.

It was.

"I got this nigga right where I want him, sis," she said to Fantasia. "If I can't get him by the end of the week it'll definitely be within the next couple of weeks. I don't see him trying to leave me anytime soon." She giggled and eyed herself in the mirror. "I fucked that nigga's brains out, and now I'm going to blow them out."

"Don't rush it," Fantasia advised. "Play it out for a month or two if you have to. Shit, get that nigga to spend some money first."

"Girl, he already talkin' about blowin' a mill on a bitch. Think I ain't gon' get that first? We from Harlem, come on, b. You know me better than that."

"Just make sure you shoot him right in his head when you do it. Give him a few extra bullets just for the fuck of it."

"He's as good as dead."

"For Janny," Fantasia said.

"For Janny."

**Epilogue

The following morning Blake was awakened by a wet thump on his bedroom floor.

He sat up and noticed that Barbie had her knees pulled up to her chest and her arms wrapped tightly around them.

Her eyes were wide and full of tears.

She was looking at Enrique, who was sitting in a wheelchair at the bedroom door smiling at the two of them in bed. A pretty Hispanic woman stood behind him.

There was blood dripping from Enrique's hand, and a severed head lay in a growing pool of blood at his feet.

"Wake up, wake up," Enrique said. "Early bird gets the worm."

"Man, what the fuck you on?" Blake said. "Don't start with that Papi-type shit."

Blake had not a clue of whose head it was, but he had a feeling it was the man responsible for the suicide bombing that now had his wife in the hospital.

********The End********

Keep reading for a sneak peek of "Bulletface 5: Drill Season"

Prologue

"That's the guy who tried to kill your wife in Indianapolis," Enrique said, gesturing toward the severed head on the floor in front of his wheelchair.

"Why in the fuck would you bring it here?!" Blake hopped out of bed, not even caring that he was stark naked, and grabbed his Glock off the nightstand. "What kinda shit you on, Enrique? You can't be doing no shit like this. You see I got my lil chick laid up in here wit' me. How you gon' roll in here with a chopped off head and just throw the muhfucka on my marble floor?"

"I could care less about your side piece. Your wife's in the hospital, facing over four hundred federal indictments, and your sorry ass missed going to see her because you've been too busy laying here fucking another woman." Enrique held up his left arm to show Blake the bandaged stomp where his left hand used to be. "See that? I lost my fucking hand, for Christ's sake. Got burns all up and down my legs. This shit isn't fun."

Shaking his head in utter disbelief and pulling on a pair of fresh Versace boxers and True Religion jeans, Blake signaled for the girl in his bed — an Atlanta stripper he knew only as Baddie Barbie — to go into the bathroom. "Shut the door behind you."

She quickly ran to the bathroom and slammed the door closed.

The Hispanic woman in back of Enrique's wheelchair laughed, as if seeing a dead man's decapitated head being dropped to the floor was the most hilarious experience of her morning.

"You're the king of cocaine now," Enrique said. "Boss of the most powerful drug cartel in history. You'd better get ready to start seeing at least a couple of heads every day if you want to stay on top. There's no room for the timid in Mexico."

"Get the fuck out of my room," Blake snapped.

"Will do." Enrique's face was one big smile. "But before I go, I thought it best to tell you not to put Indianapolis on your travel list anytime soon. Cops out there want you for questioning in a murder investigation."

The Hispanic lady behind Enrique pulled his wheelchair out of the doorway and disappeared down the hallway with him.

Blake stared at the head and tried to think of a way to dispose of it.

He also thought of the Indianapolis murder and hoped no eyewitnesses would be able to point him out as one of the gunmen...